Pretty THING

NEW YORK TIMES BESTSELLING AUTHOR

JA HUSS

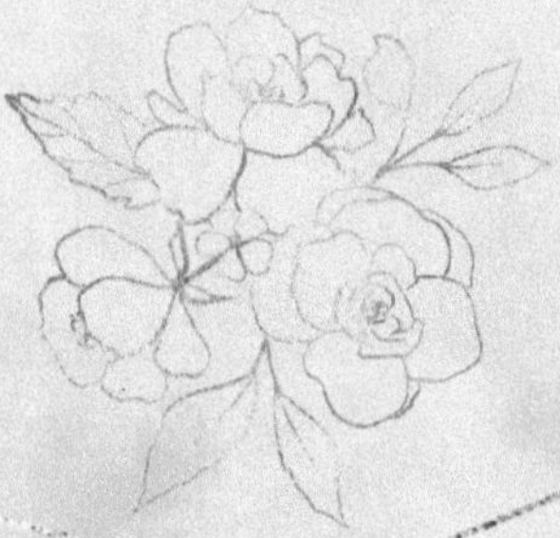

Edited by RJ Locksley
Cover Design by JA Huss
Cover photo: Sara Eirew

Pretty Thing is new sexy, brother's-best-friend romance filled with tender moments, second chances, and steamy love scenes that will make you sigh with happiness when you turn the last page!

KALI

Growing up it was always the three of us. Me, my twin brother, Kyle, and our best friend, Aiden. We were inseparable. The best of friends until I left to do my own thing in the city when I was eighteen.

Did I picture myself with Aiden from the first moment I laid eyes on him back when we were eight? Hell. Yes. I fell in love with his soul that day. And then, when we turned sixteen, I thought about other ways I could fall for him too. Grown-up ways.

But by that time he was more Kyle's friend than mine. And Kyle made damn sure we both know the rules. Anything more than friends was strictly off limits. Forever.

Still… Aiden was the only one I ever wanted.

And now Kyle is gone. Dead from a freak accident. And Aiden is still here. Looking hot as hell in his grown-up body. Looking sexy AF with those tattoos all over his muscular. Sad and in need of comfort. Just like me.

AIDEN

If you want to get technical, I was Kali's friend first, not Kyle's. She was the first thing I saw when my mom and I moved out to the suburbs when I was eight. She was a golden little pretty thing making a flower chain out of buttercups in the grass.

But that's not how Kyle saw it. "You were my friend first," was exactly what he told me every time he got an inkling that I felt something more than friendship for his twin sister. And all this time I've honored that. But now he's gone and I'm mad about that. So… maybe this is what he gets for dying on us? Maybe this is what he gets for leaving us like this?

And maybe that's how it started? Just two sad friends getting together after a funeral.

But that's not all I want from Kali. She is still that pretty thing out on the grass twirling buttercups. She is still the only girl I have eyes for.

But how do I get Kyle's blessing to fully love his sister now that he's gone?

CHAPTER ONE

It was the perfect place to grow up as a kid. Just a townhouse development out on the far edge of the farthest sprawling suburbs to most people, but to an eight-year-old this place was magical.

My mom and I always lived in apartments before that. Not nice ones, either. Dingy ones. Run-down ones with ant problems, mice problems, drunk neighbor problems. But this year I turned eight we moved out of the city because she started working for this lawyer guy.

(Yes, he did end up being my step-dad. It was one of those sappy, romantic, 'down-on-her-luck single mother finds a fucking prince who whisks her off to the magical kingdom of small-town townhouses while giving her a well-above-minimum-wage job so she can make her own choices for once' stories.)

His name is Bob. My dad, that is. And he looks like a Bob. He sounds like a Bob, he acts like a Bob and you know what? What a fucking relief, right? Because in the city the guys who were interested in my mom were all called Chad, or Todd, or Snakes. She literally dated a guy named Snakes.

So Bob Edwards was a huge step up for her.

Anyway… I'm rambling.

I'm trying to think back to the day I met them. The twins who lived across the green space from us. Like I said, this townhouse place was magical. There was grass. Like… lots of it. And all the front doors of the townhouses faced each other across this expanse of greenery. About thirty of them all lined up in a row on one side and the same number on the other side.

Off to my left were the woods and off to my right was a rock feature. Like a big pile of boulders surrounded by water—not a lot of water, enough so you could jump from the shore to the nearest boulder and clamber your way up to the peak. And there was a pump or something that made water trickle down the rocks. In the pond there were tadpoles, and frogs, and one summer there was even a turtle.

Maybe this isn't magical to some people but it was for me. I'm telling you, to a kid who had so far grown up with nothing but trashcans outside his front stoop, this was heaven. In my eight-year-old mind it felt like I'd been picked up and set down inside a whole new world. I don't know what my life would look like right now if

I had stayed in the city. Maybe I'd still be this guy, but probably not.

So the nature was cool and all, but the best thing about living in those townhouses was the twins, Kali and Kyle. Same age as me. They'd lived there all their lives so I was some exotic city boy who knew nothing about how to survive in the woods for an afternoon, or build a fort, or how to catch and raise tadpoles on your back patio, or where the wild berries grew in the summer— and they took it upon themselves to teach me their sleepy, small-town ways.

The three of us were inseparable. Ten minutes after the movers arrived I was enrolled in Kali and Kyle's school of middle-class survival.

So that's where it started.

I sigh and suddenly realize I've said all this out loud.

I'm standing at a podium on the church altar giving Kyle's eulogy. Everyone is crying. Everyone but me. I can't even look at Kali because if I do I'll lose it and I don't want to lose it. Not yet. I have to keep my shit in check until I'm done because this is my only chance to pay Kyle the respect he deserves. My last chance to honor him and let him know how much I loved him, how much I'll miss him, and how life will never be the same now that he's gone.

I was gonna say, "And now this is where it ends." That sentence is written down on the piece of paper in front of me, but I can't bring myself to say it. Because that cheats Kali out of what must come next.

A life without her twin.

It's a life unimaginable. One that should not even have to be imagined, but must. Because this is real and I want her to know that I get it, even if I can never fully get it.

So I wing it. I talk about how we grew up, and Kyle went to business school, and I went to mechanic school, and Kali moved away to chef school. And how Kyle and I opened up Rock Crawler Custom Jeeps and lived a life of testosterone-filled bliss for more than a decade.

I don't know why I think everyone is interested in this shit, but I don't care if they're not. I am. I need to retell it. Need to remind myself that life was good once.

Plus I'm trying to avoid saying that final goodbye, you know? Trying to prolong this speech so we don't all have to get into those limos, ride out to the cemetery, and throw dirt on his coffin.

Eventually I do mumble out a goodbye to my best friend and walk back to my seat.

My mom is there to wrap her hands around my upper arm and lean into me. And Bob is there to whisper, "Very nicely done, Aiden. He would've loved that eulogy." Which means a lot to me. Probably more than he realizes when he says it.

Then everything is a blur. A priest, and then me and the other dudes from the garage are carrying the casket out to the hearse, and then, before I know it, time has cheated me out of minutes and I'm standing at his grave site, throwing that handful of dirt over the top of his casket that has been defaced with decals and stickers of cars, and Jeeps, and competitions we went to—because Kyle would've loved that.

And then the next thing I know everyone but Kali and me is gone. We're just sitting there in those foldable chairs, looking at the gravesite. There's a backhoe waiting patiently not far away, ready to scoop up the rest of the dirt and cover Kyle up for good.

Kali isn't one of those sobbers, ya know. She's not hyperventilating and there's no snot running out of her nose. She just sits next to me with her hands in her lap and stares straight ahead.

I think I know what her heart feels like though, because mine feels the same way.

She's asking herself, *How will I get through the rest of this life without my twin?*

Because I'm asking myself the same thing.

She sighs, heavily. Like she's tired.

"Where are you staying?" I ask. "At home?"

I barely catch her shaking her head out of the corner of my eye. "Not staying."

"Not even one night?"

She shakes her head again. "I need to get back home."

"Why?"

"Because…" She hesitates, then whispers, "I don't know."

"You'll just have to come back next week for the will," I say.

"I don't think I'm going to that," she says. Then, for the first time today, we look directly at each other.

Kali is a pretty thing. Soft, round face, small nose, plump lips, and long, dark, wavy hair that falls over her shoulders like a cape. She's wearing a little make-up today. Eyeliner maybe, because her eyes are darker than normal. And she probably started the day with some lipstick, but it's gone now. Her black dress is basic. Nothing fancy. But she's wearing a black hat with a veil over her face. So I see her sadness through this honeycomb screen of lace and my heart sinks. Or maybe it's my stomach. I'm not sure. I just have an urge to put my arm around her, so I do.

She leans against me, slumping a little, like this is a relief.

"Remember when you and Kyle traded places for a day?"

She huffs out a small laugh and even though I can't see her face, I can picture her smile. She always had a wide, warm smile.

"Oh, God," she mutters. "Why did we do that?"

"I think it's because he wanted to wear your clothes," I say.

She laughs again. "I think it's because he wanted to trade chores that day. He was supposed to wash the car and I was supposed to sweep the patio." She tilts her head up at me, still smiling. "Guess who was out playing in the woods with you first?"

I smile back at her. "God, Kali. I've missed you. Why'd you move two hours away?"

"I dunno." She shrugs. And then she does sob. Like a little hiccup with a squeak of sadness. "I'm lying," she says. "I do know. I stayed in the city because I wanted to see what life would be like without Kyle. I wanted to live as a single for once, instead of a twin."

I pull her close to me and lean against her now too. So we can prop each other up.

"There's nothing wrong with that, ya know. Besides, I took your place anyway. Everyone calls me Kali now. Even Kyle." I laugh. Because it's true. It was a running joke in the garage that Kyle and I were so tight, I was his new twin sister.

Kali laughs with me.

Until we realize I just used Kyle's name in the present tense.

And then that ache in my heart becomes overwhelming and I sink a little further down in my chair.

Giving in to the sadness.

CHAPTER TWO

I knew this day was going to be tough. The last four days have been hell. But I was hoping that by the end of the day I'd feel something. Not relief, of course. That's not the right emotion. But… I don't know. Like I could take a breath again. Because there's been a tightness in my chest since I got the news. Like I can't inhale all the way and then, when I finally manage it, I can't exhale either. I don't know if that makes sense. I just know it hurts to breathe and my only goal right now is to learn to breathe again.

But it's not happening. I still can't seem to suck in enough air. I can't seem to stop clenching my teeth and balling my hands up into fists.

Aiden helps a little. I know this is just as hard for him as it is for me, and I can tell that last remark, which he only made to cheer me up, has cheered him down.

So I say, "I just don't know what life looks like now, ya know?"

He nods. "Yeah, believe me, I know. Monday morning we'll open the garage back up and I'll get my cup of coffee and open the bay doors, and wait for him to walk in." Aiden sighs. "And he never will, ya know? He's never gonna do that again."

"I know," I say. "I wish I hadn't moved away. I wish I'd been here this whole time. At least then I could miss him the way you do. But I'm going to go back to my apartment and wake up tomorrow and nothing will be different."

"That's not true," he says, reaching across my leg to grab my hand.

I like the way his forearm feels lying across my thigh. It's the first time he's held my hand in years. Maybe since we were little kids. And it feels good. It feels right.

"You're going to feel different every day. I know, because even though Kyle was just my best friend and not my twin, I have a space here now, you know?"

His other hand makes a fist and thumps against his chest. Right over his heart.

"It's pretty empty in there," I say. "Hollow or something."

"Yeah," Aiden agrees. "Hollow. That's exactly how I feel."

I sigh, wanting to get up and leave this fucking cemetery but unable to find the strength to do that. My parents took the limo back home and I told them I'd walk. Our townhouse isn't that far from here. About three miles, maybe. Not a great idea when I'm wearing heels, but I don't care. I'll take them off and walk barefoot like we used to do when we were kids. I just couldn't get in that car with them knowing we'd end up back at home. I don't think I can do that just yet. I'd rather walk a hundred miles right now than go home knowing Kyle will never be there with us again.

"So…" Aiden says. "What do you do in the city? I feel like we haven't talked in a long time."

"Hmmm," I say. Because it has been a while since I saw him. Our last birthday, probably. That just kills any chance of feeling better. Because my whole life I've shared a birthday with my brother and now I don't.

"You have a job, of course," he says. Prodding me to talk.

"Yes," I say. "I'm the head chef now at Bistecca del Bosco."

"Nice," he says.

I shrug. "I guess."

"You don't like it?"

"Not really."

"Then do something else," he says, like this is so simple.

I laugh. Not a happy laugh but a 'yeah, right' laugh. "Cooking just isn't as fun as I thought it'd be. I mean, I always wanted to be a baker, for one thing. But there's no money in baking. And the only other thing I really know how to do is work on those stupid Jeeps."

"Stupid Jeeps," Aiden echoes. Sadly, I might add. Because that's how Kyle died. Rock-crawling out in Utah. The Jeep flipped over backwards and crushed him. We had to have one of those half-open caskets because he was not in good shape from the chest down from what they tell me.

"I should've gone to business school with him," I say.

Aiden just squeezes my hand.

"I don't know how you can even look at them," I say.

"Who?"

"The fucking Jeeps," I say, turning my head so I can meet his gaze.

He presses his lips together and frowns. "He was doing what he loved, Kali."

"Yeah, and now he's dead."

"The Jeep didn't do this," he says. "He made a mistake. People do that, ya know. Because they're people."

"Are you going to sell the place?" I ask.

"Do you think I should sell the place?"

"Why do you care what I think?"

"Because he probably left you his share in the will."

"Oh," I say. "I hadn't thought of that."

Aiden sighs. "Let's talk about something else."

"Like how we're going to get home?" I huff another fake laugh. "Because everyone is gone and I know that the backhoe operator is probably well-schooled in graveside etiquette, but I'm pretty sure he's giving us the stink-eye right now."

Aiden looks around the cemetery. It's on a hillside on the edge of town. And there's a nice view of the mountains from where we're sitting. The sun is just beginning to set and this day is almost over.

"We can just walk," he says. "Your house isn't that far away. People are probably wondering where we're at."

"I can't do that," I say. "I just can't. I'm not going back there for some… some stupid… whatever it is. It feels like a party. Why do people want to eat and drink after a funeral? It makes no sense to me."

"Just… to remember him. And have a chance to share memories?"

I shake my head a little and huff out some air.

"I'll call a car," he says, letting go of my hand to reach for his phone.

But I grab his hand back and say, "No. I can walk just fine. I just can't go back to the house and listen politely as people try to console me. Or worse, expect me to console them. I don't care if it's rude. I just lost my twin and I'm not in the mood to hear how sorry everyone is for my loss."

"Oh," Aiden says, understanding me. Like the idea of ditching the reception never entered his mind. "Well, I'll walk you to your car and then make excuses for you."

"You will?" I ask, looking at him again. Like… really looking at him. His blue-green eyes are blurry today. Like the tropical ocean they usually resemble has been muddied with silt. His hair is dark and cropped short everywhere but on top near the front. So that every time he bows his head it tumbles down over his face in loose curls.

His nose is straight, even though I know it was broken once when he was sixteen and Kyle accidentally hit him with a wrench when they were working on their first Jeep together. I went to the hospital with them, holding a cloth over Aiden's face as Kyle said, "Sorry, dude. Sorry, dude," over and over again. But he had surgery to fix it a few days later so it's straight now.

He grins at me, noticing I'm looking at him. His smile is wide and he always shows teeth. Even when he's angry, he'll smile and show teeth. Like a dog getting ready to attack.

His jaw is square and clean-shaven. Usually he's got days' worth of stubble on that chin. And once, when he was seventeen, he grew a goatee.

That makes me laugh.

"What?" he asks, looking into my eyes.

And then we talk about his goatee. And of course, he has to bring up that time I tried to wax my bikini area the day before we went out to the lake for a long weekend and I couldn't even wear my bathing suit because I had these god-awful red marks all over my upper thighs.

Pretty soon we're laughing about the time Aiden shaved Kyle's head when he passed out drunk one New Year's Eve and how Kyle got back at him the next year by taking pictures of Aiden with a dildo in his mouth.

Before we know it the sun has set. The backhoe guy is lugging out lights and setting them up around us and every chair but the two we're sitting in has been collected and stacked onto the back of a little tractor.

Then we're sad again because we realize we've been here for hours, laughing, and smiling, and having a pretty good time. Forgetting that Kyle's dead body is lying just a few feet away.

"Hey," Aiden says. "You ready to get out of here?"

I sigh, hesitating. Because I'm not. Not really. Walking away from Kyle's grave means they're going to fill it up. And then he'll really be gone.

"Come on," Aiden says, standing up and taking my hand. He pulls me to my feet and I slip my shoes off, readying myself for the long walk home.

He takes them from me, holding them in one hand while holding me in the other, and leads me across the cemetery and down the hill to the town.

CHAPTER THREE

We walk through the gates of the cemetery holding hands. It feels wrong in many ways. For one, I had a crush on Kali when I was a kid. I got a little sappy, trying to carry her books home from school and shit like that. So Kyle took me aside in the woods one day and said, "You're my best friend, but if you ever try to hold my sister's books again, I'll punch you in the eye."

End of Aiden's crush on Kali. Like, needle-scratching-across-an-old-record kind of full stop.

Except it wasn't the end. It was just the beginning.

I admit, I jerked off to the image of Kali's face more times than I can count back when I was a teenager. And yeah, there was that time I saw her naked. She was getting out of the shower and a bunch of us guys were hanging out in Kyle's living room and I just so happened to be coming up the steps to grab my jacket out of Kyle's room and there she was with her door cracked open a little, looking through a pile of clothes on her bed.

She didn't know I was there right away. Took her time finding a shirt and a pair of shorts as I peeked at her like a pervert. Then when she looked up and saw me, she smiled. For a second I was like… *OK. She's naked and smiling at me. She probably wants me.* I even got a little hard. I was seventeen. You can't stop that shit when you're seventeen.

But then she walked over to the door. Not even embarrassed or anything. Just walked over to me with her perfect tits and nicely groomed pussy. She opened the door a little wider and yelled, "Kyle! Aiden's upstairs peeking in my room!"

There was a bunch of, "What?" "What?" "What'd she say?" from all the guys downstairs.

Which, gotta be honest, made me panic a little. But then she kneed me in the nuts and by the time they all came upstairs to see what was happening Kali was safely behind her locked door and I was writhing on the ground like an idiot.

Kyle did one of those, "You're an asshole," laughs guys do when they know you deserve another punch in the eye but just got something better. Then he walked away.

But he did make a point later of telling me if I ever peeked at his sister again, he'd sneak into my bedroom at night and cut off my dick.

So holding her hand after his funeral is definitely up there with peeking at her naked when she was seventeen.

I can practically hear him now. "Aiden, you asshole. I've warned you twice already. I'm not gonna waste time with words, OK? I'm just gonna knock your fucking teeth out."

But I don't let go of her hand.

He's not here, right? *Joke's on you, dickface. I guess that's what you get for leaving me alone with her.*

Kali groans as we walk down the big hill into town. Calling it a town is a bit much. Back when they built our little townhome community this place was an up-and-coming suburb. The city would eventually sprawl out and then it wouldn't be so far away from everything.

But that's not how it turned out. The urban sprawl ended up going west instead of east so our town is still the same as it was when we were kids.

Kyle and I came back here to set up our shop after school. Actually, I came first—he was in business school and took two more years to finish. So I rented an old garage with an apartment upstairs and that's where I've lived ever since.

It was a total dump back then but it's really nice now. We expanded the building several years ago and added three more bays. So we now have five full-time mechanics, including Kyle and me, an office manager named Karen, and a couple of kids from the mechanic school who work there for their internship.

It's on a side street in the middle of town. And by middle I mean at the bottom of the hill just next to the river. Which is pretty much where everything is in this town that's not really a town. One real cross street with a few side streets on either side of the river. And we only have two stoplights. Both of them are at the top of the hills that flank the town. Technically we have three stoplights if you count the one in front of the fire station, but that one only works if there's a fire and the engines need to get out onto the two-lane highway.

"Why are you groaning?" I ask Kali. Because she just did it again.

"There's stones on the sidewalk," she says, tiptoeing her way around the stones.

I stop us and turn my back to her. "Get on," I say. "I'll carry you like the old days."

She laughs a little. "You never carried me on your back in your life."

Truth. Kyle would've killed me. He was the one who always did that.

But you're not here, are you? I silently ask him. *So that's what you get for leaving us alone, jerkoff. I guess if you really wanted to keep me away from your sister you'd have stuck around.*

"I know," I say. "But I can't stand your whining and groaning. Now get on."

I look over my shoulder at her. Daring her to say no. Or maybe just glaring at her, because there's a sudden rush of anger inside me. Anger that Kyle isn't here to stop me. Anger that maybe I want to do more to his sister than just hold her hand and give her a piggy-back ride.

That maybe I want to take her home.

And I know I can. No one's gonna stop me but her.

"Fine," she says, placing her hands on my shoulder. She jumps and I catch her, dropping her shoes in the process.

"Oh, shit," she says as I hike her up on my back. Just the feeling of her legs wrapped around me gets me hard.

And I think to myself, *Aiden, what the fuck is wrong with you? Her brother has been dead four days and you're already planning to eat the forbidden fruit.*

Sure, I agree that makes me a Grade-A douchebag. But I don't care.

You're not here, ha!

I just bend down next to her shoes and say, "Grab 'em," and then stand back up once she's got them in her hand. "Should we run?" I ask her.

"No." She laughs.

But I'm already running. And she's bouncing on my back, laughing, and it's a hot summer night with no wind, so the wind I make feels cool, and good, and soothing.

She starts to slip and I know this whole break in the sadness has a lifetime limit of maybe ten more seconds, but I make the most of those ten seconds by heading towards a large green lawn along the side of a big old house that is actually a real estate office, and fall into the grass with her, rolling around until Kali's on her back and I'm propped up over top of her, looking down into her eyes.

She smiles. No teeth. Like she's waiting. Like maybe she's been waiting her whole life for this moment.

I lean down. Slow enough that she has time to make a decision. But fast enough that I don't lose my nerve. And I kiss her on the lips.

Kali and Aiden's first kiss. Walking home from Kyle's funeral.

I pull back immediately and she lets out a long breath of air. Fingertips touching her lips like she can't believe I just did that.

"Sorry," I say. "I just couldn't stop myself."

She nods at me, silent. The moon is out now. Shining down into her eyes. Then she says, "OK."

"Yeah?" I ask, knowing full well she wasn't giving me permission. Just agreeing with my statement about not being able to stop. So I'm leading her on here, but I don't care.

"Sure," she says, going down the path to hell with me. Willingly.

I put my hand on her thigh and slide it up her leg before I come to my senses and stop.

She tilts her head at me, questioning.

"You should stay the night at my place. Get drunk with me. Talk about old times and shit like that."

Shit like that meaning… *All those times I wanted to jump your bones and never could, but now I can, so I'm using this as an excuse to take you home, and put you in my bed, then fuck your brains out because I'm sad. And you're sad. And there's no one here to stop us now because he's the reason we're sad.*

"OK," she says again.

And again, I respond, "Yeah?"

And she nods.

Yes.

I roll off her and get to my feet, extending my hand down to her. She takes it and I pull her up in one smooth motion. She's small compared to me. Only about five foot six, maybe. And pulling her up, she is light too. Like a feather.

We stand there on the side lawn between the real estate office house and Mrs. Cranston's driveway, under the glow of a single yellow streetlight, and look for something in each other's eyes.

I'm looking for solace and I think she is too.

So I say, "Come on. We can cut through the back yard." And then we are eight years old again. I'm leading her through Mrs. Cranston's back yard, half expecting her to open her window and yell at us to stop cutting through her yard because we're making a path in her grass.

But Mrs. Cranston doesn't live here anymore. She lives up the hill now. One of Kyle's new neighbors. Plus it's night. Jack and Marie Lesser, who live here now, are probably over at Kyle and Kali's parents' house for the reception.

And we are not eight, anyway. We are both just a couple of sad, thirty-somethings who used to be someone else. And we'd give anything to be those kids again, but of course, that's impossible.

But maybe for one night we can pretend.

CHAPTER FOUR

He leads me through Mrs. Cranston's yard and for some stupid, inexplicable reason I feel like I'm being bad. I tell myself that it's because we're not supposed to do this. Cut through her yard. She hates it. And if she saw us, she'd open a window, and shake her fist, and complain that the neighborhood is going to hell.

I laugh out loud.

"What's funny?" Aiden asks, swiping a stray branch from the old apple tree aside so I can slip through the low hedge that surrounds the back edge of the property and leads to the back alley behind the Jeep shop.

Safely on the other side I feel a wave of relief. Some leftover emotion from twenty-five years ago. "Mrs. Cranston would kill us if she caught us."

"Oh," Aiden says. "You don't know?"

"Know what?"

"She died a couple years back. Jack and Marie Lesser live here now."

"Oh," I say, stopping in my tracks. For some reason this hits me hard. Maybe because I didn't know and I should've. Should've shown up for her funeral, at least. Or maybe because it's a symptom of why I'm standing here in this alley with Aiden, on my way to his apartment, when I should be at my parents' house celebrating my twin brother's life.

"What's wrong?" Aiden asks.

"I dunno," I say, letting go of his hand and turning my back to him. "Maybe we shouldn't do this?"

"What are we doing?" he asks.

I turn back to him and shrug. "What *are* we doing?"

"Hmm," he says, rubbing his jaw with his hand. He does that a lot. It's something I like about him. And usually there's some stubble there so there's a very faint, very soft, scratching noise.

But not tonight.

"We could get drunk," he offers. "We could get shit-faced drunk and talk about old times." He pauses for a moment, then adds, "Have we ever gotten drunk together?"

I shake my head. "No," I say. "Kyle… you know."

Kyle would never let me get drunk in front of him. In fact, after we graduated high school and went our separate ways, it was never the same again. It was never the three of us anymore. It was those two, and then me, off to the side.

"Yeah. OK. You want me to drive you home?" he asks. Smiling, but for the first time I can ever remember, there's no teeth. Not a real smile.

"Yeah," I say. "That's probably a good idea."

He nods. He understands. Then sighs and looks at my shoes in my hand. "You should put those on. Lots of stones in the alley."

I look down at them too, then back at him. I shrug. "How about another ride?" I say. "For old times' sake?"

He says, "Hmmm," because he knows damn well that he was never the one to carry me on his back. Kyle was. "Yeah, why not."

He turns his back to me and I jump on, laughing again. The sad memories fading a little.

I feel guilty about that, but you know what? Kyle should feel guilty too. For liking that stupid rock crawling. For making a mistake. For getting crushed to death by a goddamned Jeep.

See, Kyle? I say silently. *This is what you get for leaving me.*

Because in those few moments it takes to walk down the alley to the back door of Rock Crawler Custom Jeeps, I change my mind again. Because if I get in Aiden's car and let him drop me off at mine, I will probably go back to the city and never see him again. It's a stupid idea because I'll come home for holidays and stuff and Aiden's parents live right across the greenspace from mine. But I'll never really have another reason to see Aiden again. I'll never be able to stop by the shop and steal secret glances at him while pretending to be there to talk to Kyle. Not that I've done that over the years, but it was always a possibility and now it's not.

"You know what?" I say, once Aiden sets me down so he can find his keys.

"What?" he says, only half listening as he sticks the key in the lock and opens the door.

"I changed my mind. I would like to get drunk."

This time the smile does have teeth. And maybe in more ways than one. "Yeah?" he asks. And I feel like this has been our conversation the whole night. Feeling things, then forgetting things, then feeling things again. Not really certain we know what we're doing, but then again, not really caring.

I nod anyway. "Yup," I say, so we can change the dialog from uncertainty to certainty. "Get me good and drunk, Aiden Edwards. Because tonight, of all nights, I need it."

I need you too, I don't add. Because that feels like crossing a line and I'm not ready to go there.

Yet.

"I can't think of a single fucking thing I'd rather do right now, Kali Anderson. Now be careful, this place is a fucking mess."

And then he takes my hand and doesn't turn on the lights. Just leads me through the shop, pretending to carefully pick his way around massive tool chests, and Jeeps up on lifts, and all that other stuff that comes with a garage like this.

But there's a part of me that knows better. Knows that this place is spotless and he knows it just as well in the dark as he does in the light. That he just wants to keep hold of my hand and lead me.

Of course, I don't say any of that. Because that's what I want too.

His apartment is on the second floor and to get to it you have to go down a long hallway away from the garage. If we'd come to the shop from the front we'd have entered through a separate entrance on the outside. But we didn't.

He stops at the stairs and says, "You go first. That way if you fall I can catch you."

I huff out a laugh. Because I'm quite capable of walking up steps. But then I realize two things.

One. I've never been up here before. And two. The steps are steep. Like whoever built them did so a hundred years ago before there were regulations.

They're also narrow. But there's two hand rails on either side and I grip them going up. Aiden is very close behind me. Almost touching me. In fact, I can feel his knees brushing up against the hem of my dress with each step. He grips the rails too, because every few steps I leave my hands in place a moment too long and his fingers brush against mine.

These small things send a shiver up my spine and make my skin burst out in goosebumps. Like I'm sixteen again and not thirty-four.

Has he always affected me this way? Or am I feeling this way because Kyle is gone now and Aiden is all I have left?

Hard to tell. A part of me has always dreamed about being with Aiden. But the other part knew that came with consequences. So maybe there were a few daydreams. A few what-if scenarios. But until now I knew that's all they'd ever be.

Until now Aiden wasn't all I had left. But do I care if that's why I'm doing this?

Not really.

The landing at the top of the stairs is very small and cramped. Aiden has to reach past me to unlock his door. And I wonder for a second if this is his typical move when he brings girls home to his apartment?

You go first, I imagine him telling these interloper girls. *So I can push you up against the door a little before we even get inside.*

I let out a breath just as Aiden opens the door, and he says, "You OK?"

"Yup." I lie. I'm not OK but I really want to be.

"Let me find a light."

He pushes past me, hands on my hips as he maneuvers. And I think… *Yup. This is Aiden Edwards' little one-night-stand move number one.*

But then his hands are gone and I miss them. I want them back.

The lights flick on and he's got his back to me, looking down at his feet.

"You OK?" It's my turn to ask.

He turns and smiles. With teeth. So a normal one, and I take his word on that. "What do you drink, Kali? I have no idea."

"Why… martinis and mimosas, of course."

He belts out a laugh that's too loud, but also too genuine to care. "Whiskey it is."

"Hmm." I laugh too. Lips pressed together. "I guess you do know me."

He walks over to the kitchen, taking his suit coat off as he goes. Tossing it over the back of a chair. "Not as well as I'd like," he quips.

Then he sucks in a deep breath and pauses for a moment as he's reaching to open a cabinet.

He looks over his shoulder and says, "That's not why you're here."

"Why am I here?" I ask.

He shrugs, grabs the bottle, then two short glasses, and says, "Lots of reasons."

"Name a few, "I say. Because I don't know why I'm really here and I desperately *want* to know. And I also want to know if I'm reading him right.

I think we're going to have sex tonight. I wouldn't call it planned, but it's not gonna be spontaneous either.

"Memories," he says, pouring some whiskey into a glass. Then he pauses. "I don't really know you anymore, Kali. And for some reason that really fucking bothers me tonight." He pours the other glass, turns and walks over to me, then hands me mine. "Cheers," he says. "To Kyle. Not just a best friend, but a brother."

I just stare at him for a second. Because that was a loaded statement.

Did he say that because I'm the sister and he's the best friend?

Or did he say that because *he's* like a brother to me too, and what we're going to do tonight is wrong on many levels?

But once I take a sip I decide I don't care.

I hate this day and I want Aiden Edwards to be the person who wipes it all away.

CHAPTER FIVE

I down the whiskey in one gulp. And you know why? Because that's how we drink it, Kyle and I. That's how we get down to business when we decide to get drunk.

Kali takes a sip and I shake my head and laugh. "Oh, fuck that," I say. "Fuck that."

"Fuck what? What are you talking about?"

"You don't get to sip it," I say, suddenly feeling angry. "Fucking down it, Kali. Or you can't drink with me."

"What?" She laughs.

"I'm fuckin' serious," I say. And I am. I don't know why, or where this is coming from, I'm just suddenly pissed off. "Down it or get out."

"Prick," she says. But she tilts the glass to her lips and swallows it all. She hands it back to me. "Fill me up, asshole."

And suddenly, I'm better. God, what is wrong with me tonight? I'm like a fuckin' teenage girl with all the goddamned emotions I'm feeling. But I walk into the kitchen, grab the bottle and come back out into the living room, pointing it at the couch. "Take a seat, little sister. We're gonna do this proper."

"Proper, huh?" And she makes a face. "I'm not your sister."

"You are now," I say, then regret it. *Because no, Aiden, that's not right.* "I mean, you know."

"I know what you mean," she says, taking a seat on the couch and patting the cushion next to her. "Sit down and pour."

I grin at her and take a seat. Purposefully close, but not too close so I'm obvious. I've wanted to kiss her my entire life and I finally take the chance and it's… not good enough. I need a do-over.

But that can wait. We've got whiskey to drink first. I pour it into her glass as she holds it, then refill mine and set the bottle down.

"You know these are doubles, right?" she says, staring at the level in her glass. "We should be taking shots if you want to drink like this."

"Tonight," I say, clinking my glass to hers, "tonight we drink like you're Kyle and not Kali."

"Mmm-hmmm," she hums. "I get it. Trying to get me drunk, are you? So you can kiss me again?" She smiles as she lifts her glass to her lips. Pauses, then tips her head back and downs it.

I wait, my glass half lifted to my lips, and look at her, serious again. "Yeah," I say. "So I can kiss you again and not think about how Kyle would kick my ass if he were here."

I down my drink and place it on the coffee table.

"Well, you know what?" Kali says.

"Hmm?"

"He's not here, is he?" She pours us each another two fingers, and holds her glass up to the ceiling. "Fuck you, Kyle. Fuck you for not being here. How you like that, brother? Feels good, right? To be left out, and left behind." Then she looks at me and says, "I'm gonna kiss him back next time." And then she downs her drink.

I smile, lift my glass up to the ceiling, and say, "Yeah, fuck you, Kyle." And down mine too.

Kali is already pouring again. We just did six shots in the span of two minutes and yeah, I can hold my fucking whiskey, but that's a lot of alcohol flooding my system right now.

"You know what the best part is?" Kali asks, handing me another double.

I turn my body to the side a little and lean back into the cushions. Her hair is kind of a mess right now. A little bit in her face, not smooth and sleek like it normally is. Just haphazardly framing her cheeks like an unruly tangle of underbrush.

My fingers reach out, like they have a mind of their own, and brush some of it away from her cheek. "Hmm?" I ask. "What's the best part, Kal?"

"Kal." She snorts. "God, it's been years since you called me that."

"Kal," I say, brushing my knuckles down her cheek, a part of me unable to believe I have permission to do this, another part of me wondering why the hell I waited for Kyle to die before I did it. "Tell me."

"Drink first," she says.

I shrug, down the drink, and set the glass down on the coffee table.

She smiles with the glass up to her lips, then downs it and slams hers on the table next to mine, like we're at a bar and not my apartment.

"OK," she says, wiping the glistening droplets of alcohol off her lips. "This is the best part. You ready?"

"You're already drunk," I say, laughing.

She slaps my leg, laughing too. "I am not. I'm just… feeling better. Funny how eight shots of whiskey can do that for you."

"Jesus Christ. Only eight?" I joke. "We need two more before I can hear the best part."

"Pour," she says.

I do. I pour a little extra this time. Three shots.

She notices, but takes the glass anyway, then says, "Challenge accepted, Aiden Edwards."

We down it all, at the same time, then both of us come up for air, coughing like maniacs.

"Oh, shit!" She giggles. "I'm drunk. I've been here ten minutes—"

"Eight," I correct her with a finger point.

"—eight minutes and I'm shit-faced!"

"Technically," I say, "you're only half shit-faced. Because most of that has not hit you yet."

"I'm in trouble," she say. Then bursts out laughing.

I reach over, like… I dunno why. It's instinct, maybe. Or wishful thinking. Or twenty-six years of pent-up desire. But I reach over, place my hand on her cheek and turn her towards me. She goes quiet and still in that moment. Like she knows what I'm gonna do.

And she does. Because when I kiss her, she kisses me back.

This time it's everything last time wasn't. It's heated, not sad. Open-mouthed, not closed. And our tongues are sweet with the taste of whiskey as they tangle together.

She backs off, just a little bit, and says, "You still wanna know the best part?"

I nod my head and say, "Mmmm," as I kiss her again.

She dips her head down and says, "The best part is… I think… maybe… I have always wanted this. I once told Kyle that I liked you."

"When?" I ask, too quickly.

"Mmmm?" She rolls her eyes up, like she's thinking. "Fourteen, I think. Yeah. I was fourteen. And it was Christmas Eve. And you got me—"

"A silver locket," I say, remembering that night. "And I put my picture in there." I laugh, thinking back on that memory. "And Kyle was pissed. He ripped it off your neck and threw it away."

It was a joke. I wasn't really trying to get Kali to like me. I vaguely remember Kyle and I having a conversation about girls the week before Christmas. About how we could make them like us and get ourselves some girlfriends. And he came up with this stupid locket idea to get them all melty. So I did that—

I bought Kali that locket and put my picture in it as an inside joke between Kyle and me.

A stupid, thoughtless teenage-boy move if ever there was one.

But it definitely got his attention.

"Do you know," Kali says, shaking her head and closing her eyes like she can't believe she's gonna say this, "do you know that I took it out of the trash and kept that locket under my pillow for four years?"

I picture her doing this. "You did?"

"Mmmm-hmm," she says. "I did. After everyone left that night and Kyle was asleep. I went down into the kitchen and poked around in all the trash until I found it, and then I cleaned it up, and took it upstairs and held it in my hand all night long. And from that night forward, I had you with me every time I fell asleep."

"Jesus," I say. "I never knew."

"But anyway," she says, waving her hand in the air to clear that memory. "The best part of all this is… that time I told Kyle I liked you, he said…"

She stops. And she stares at me. Her eyes begin to water.

"What?" I ask her, sliding my hand around her waist. And not to make a move, either. Just to comfort her.

Because all of the day's sadness is about to come pouring out.

"He said, 'The day you get with Aiden is the day I die.'" And then she laughs. "But we're three days late, so I guess he wins."

"No," I say, leaning in to her again. "He lost, Kal. We're the only ones who have a chance to win now."

She meets me halfway this time. Maybe even more than halfway. Because her lips find mine instead of mine finding hers.

But this time is different in another way too. Because her hand is on my leg, sliding up my thigh, and resting on my cock. I've been getting hard, a little bit at a time, ever since we kissed outside. But now the blood rushes in and filled me up as she squeezes.

And I know for certain that we're going to do this.

Maybe there'll be regrets tomorrow, maybe not. Maybe Kyle is looking on us yelling and screaming to stop, but we don't care.

Because Kali is right. That asshole went and died on us, so fuck him and his rules. Fuck him. I'm gonna fuck his sister tonight.

And I'm not even gonna feel bad while I do it.

CHAPTER SIX

A part of me understands exactly what's happening.

We drank those shots so quick because we just needed an excuse, that's all. We need this tonight because we're all that's left of our little trio. Kyle is never coming back. He can never walk in on us. Can never get mad at us. Can never do anything, ever again.

I need Aiden to touch me everywhere, all at once. I need it like I need water, or food, or my dead brother back.

"I need you," I whisper into our kiss.

"I know," he whispers back. "I need you too."

I'm just a replacement, and so is he. We're sad. We're mad. We're missing our missing part. And the worst thing is, we don't care. We're using each other to get through this night and we don't even care.

My hand is on his cock and I can't help but imagine what it will look like once I pull it out. Some people might think a cock is a cock is a cock. But that's definitely not been my experience. Some are much better than others. And I have a feeling Aiden's is going to be spectacular.

He saw me once. Naked, that is. I was getting out of the shower and I heard Aiden tell Kyle that he left his jacket up in his bedroom. I heard him coming up the stairs.

So I dropped my towel and bent over the bed, pretending to look for clothes.

I knew he'd peek. I knew it. Hell, looking back at it now, I realize I was posing for him. But back then I didn't understand sex. I just felt a thrill at the idea he'd see me.

Of course, I made a big deal about it. Kneed him in the nuts. But that was for Kyle's benefit. I knew if there was ever anything real between Aiden and me that Kyle would not be his friend. And the three of us, that's what was important back then.

So even though I set Aiden up that day, and I wanted him, I had to make things right with Kyle before it was over.

I regret that, I realize.

Aiden's hand slips under my dress in the same moment I reach for the button on his slacks. I pop it, dragging the zipper down. And my hand is so eager to wrap itself around his shaft, I barely notice that his fingers are pressing into my pussy, right through my panties, until he hits my clit and I make a little squeal.

"Hmmm," he murmurs as we continue to kiss. "You like that?"

"I do," I hum back. I can taste the whiskey on his lips and I like it because it lets me know what this is.

One drunken encounter.

Nothing more.

Nothing less.

Just a few hours of fucking my brother's best friend so I can live through the night and see another sunrise.

Because I need that. I really do. I can't go on without Aiden tonight.

Aiden is tugging on my panties now. And I'm tugging on his cock. I already have it out of his underwear.

"Take these off," he says, still tugging.

I don't want to let go of him. I want to put his cock in my mouth and suck him until he blows, but first things first.

So I let go and ease my hips up. He's on his knees in front of me in an instant, dragging my panties down my legs. He throws them over his shoulder and places each of his hands on my knees, spreading me open wide as I lift my dress up so he can see me.

"Oh, God," he murmurs, when I reach down between my legs and begin playing with myself.

There's a part of me that aches for the younger us. A part of me that wishes we'd done this a long time ago. Back when neither of us knew what we were doing. Back when we were shy, and inexperienced.

But there's another part—the dirty part—that's glad we waited because there will be no fumbling around, no hesitations, no embarrassment. It's just drunk, sad sex and nothing more.

I stick my finger inside my pussy and look at him with heavy eyes. His are hooded as well. Filled with lust.

"Kali," he whispers. And just hearing my name makes me more excited. "Tell me what you like," he says. "We only get one shot at this, you know that, right? So let's make the most of it. Tell me how you like it."

He's right. One shot. One night and then this is over. I go back to the city, he stays here. That's it.

So I say, "Eat me out," and open my pussy lips for him. Flicking my clit back and forth with my middle finger.

He glances down, then back up at me with a wild, hungry grin.

I place my other hand on his head and push him into position. His mouth covers my clit as I tangle my fingertips into that tousled, too-long hair of his that covers his eyes, and for a moment I think… *Oh, that's what that unruly mess of waves is for.*

To hold his face between my legs as he licks me.

Then I grin, and before I know what I'm doing, I'm laughing.

He tips his head up, still eating me out, and squints his eyes. Like… *What's so funny?*

"Nothing," I whisper, my voice hoarse and deep. "I'm just imagining all the girls you eat out using this bit of hair to hold you in place and never let you stop."

He laughs too, then comes up, even though I'm pushing down, and says, "You are the only one who's ever done that, Kali."

And then he dives back down. And I don't care if he's lying. I lean my head back, position my body down on the couch cushions a little more, and enjoy it.

Both hands on his head now. Hips grinding against his face. I am eager to show him how sexual I can be. I don't know why. I just want him to know that I'm a woman now, not a kid. I'm not his sister, I'm his friend. And if we want to do this, we can.

Fuck Kyle.

He fucked us, didn't he? So now we get to fuck each other. It's only fair.

I think I might be drunk. Because that made perfect sense and no sense at all.

"Kali," Aiden moans again.

He is licking, and sucking, and using his fingers to penetrate me. And I swear to God, I'm not usually one to get off so quick, but I feel it building.

Just as I think that Aiden pulls away.

"Nooo," I complain.

He drags the back of his hand across his mouth, looking at me with an expression of pure hunger. "Not yet," he says. "I'll get you off like that later, if you want. But this first time, no way. I want to be inside you."

His pants are open and the front of his shirt is hanging over his cock, but the rest of it is still tucked in. He pulls it out and starts unbuttoning his shirt from the bottom up, giving me little peeks, first of his long, hard cock, then of his muscled abs.

I try to recall the last time I saw Aiden without a shirt and come up with… more than a decade ago. And he didn't look like this back then, that's for sure. Still kinda skinny. Lean, but not overly muscular. The years have added weight to him in all the right places.

"Oh, my God," I yell.

"Problem?" he asks, still messing with the second cuff.

"Take off that fucking shirt before I rip it off you!"

"Eager much, Kali?" He winks.

"Yes," I say. "I am. I've been picturing this since I was fourteen and—"

"What?"

"You heard me," I say. "You had to know I had a thing for you back then."

"When?" he asks, unknotting his tie and whipping it through his collar.

"Who cares?" I say. "Are we going to do this—"

"Whoa, whoa, whoa," he says, flat palm motioning me to calm down. "We've got time, OK? I want you too, but just… enjoy it a little, Kal."

"I'm enjoying it," I say. What I don't say, and actually needs to be said, is that we don't have time. This is a one-night thing. That's it. And yeah, it's still early, but I want the full Aiden experience before I walk out that door and never come back. That means him eating my pussy until I come on his face, me sucking his cock until he comes in my throat, and me fucking him every way I can think of.

He stands up, kicking off his shoes. Then drops his pants and underwear and stands there in his dark socks, grinning at me. "What do you think? Leave the socks on?"

"You're dumb." I laugh. "Take them off."

"Take off your dress," he counters.

I am whipping that thing over my head before he even finishes asking. Fuck the zipper. This one slides over easy and two seconds later I'm throwing it in the general direction of my panties and unhooking my bra, which I drop to the floor at his feet.

He sits down on the couch next to me and pats his leg. "Climb into my lap."

I swing my leg over, making sure that my pussy brushes against his hard cock, and place both hands on his shoulders as I realize something obvious, but new. "You have tattoos. Jesus. How long has it been since I saw you in short sleeves?"

"Kali," he says, voice deep and gruff. "I've seen you like four times in the past decade. Did you not even miss me?"

"That's not true," I say, looking back up at his face. "I see you every Christmas Eve."

He shakes his head. "No. Last year you were on a trip, the year before we hung out, but only at your parents' party. The year before that—"

"OK, fine," I say. "I've been gone a lot." I force a smile. Because I have a feeling he resents me for this. "But I'm here now."

"Yes," he says. "You are." He cocks his head at me, his hands sliding around my hips to squeeze my ass cheeks. "But now I'm wondering why."

CHAPTER SEVEN

I know why. It's a dumb statement. We both know why this is happening.

Kali sighs a little. Her shoulders slump and her head lowers with them. "I'm not using you," she says.

"Good," I say. "Because I'm not using you either."

"I've always liked you. And if you'd like to talk about that someday, we can. But…" She looks at me. Places her hands on the sides of my face. Blinks twice. "Not tonight, OK? Can we just not think too hard about it?"

It, meaning the sex. Or maybe the funeral. I'm not sure.

I decide to say nothing in response. I'm drunk, I'm sad, I'm horny, and I've got Kali Anderson sitting in my lap.

And we're naked.

"Come here," I say, placing my hands on her head. "I want to kiss you for a while."

She smiles into the kiss that comes next. It's a nice kiss. A slow kiss. One where our mouths fit together perfectly, and move just the right way, and there's nothing awkward or distracting about it. It's just nice.

After a little bit of that I find myself thinking too hard again.

Maybe slow and careful is a bad thing? Maybe what we really need tonight is something hard, and angry, and quick?

She reaches down between her legs and begins playing with herself again. Rubbing her pussy with the flat tips of her fingers as she stares into my eyes.

Yeah. Slow and careful is for another night.

I reach down and take my cock in my hand. Pulling and tugging on it. I'm already fully erect but there's something intimate about masturbating in front of someone. And doing it together is even hotter.

Her other hand rests on my shoulder and a chill rises up my spine.

This girl. This pretty thing I've known almost my whole life. She is the dream girl. She is the one I've always wanted. She might even be the one I've always loved.

But I get a sick, sick feeling in my stomach at that thought.

Don't think about it, Aiden. Not tonight. If you want to have an existential crisis over your choice of best friends, do it tomorrow. Or next week, or next year. Hell, maybe that's a philosophical question that never needs to be answered?

"How do you like it?" I ask her, pushing my wandering thoughts aside. I want to be with her right now, not the swirling doubts and questions in my head.

"With you?" she says. Her words slur just a little bit, reminding me that we just downed eleven shots. "I don't care."

"You don't care?" I ask. Jesus. What is wrong with me? Why am I talking?

"Why are we talking?" she asks. "We're supposed to be… you know. Fucking."

I slide my hands down to her shoulders, then down to her breasts and cup them. She has always had nice tits and they look just as good tonight as they did back when she was seventeen.

"I like that," she murmurs. Her hand on my shoulder slides down to my chest. Then she curls her fingers and brushes them back and forth across my nipple.

That chill again. It rides all the way up my spine.

It's telling me to be careful but I don't feel like listening anymore.

I pull her hand away from between her legs and say, "That's my job," as I flatten my fingers across her lower belly and slip my thumb down onto her clit.

She hisses in a breath between her teeth when I begin rubbing her clit and then closes her eyes. "Yes," she says. "It is."

I could make this end. Not by saying no, but by saying yes. Just put my cock inside her, fuck her till we come, and then take her to bed and fall asleep.

But something stops me.

"Don't stop," she whispers, reaching down to push my hand off my cock. She grabs it in her palm, squeezing and tugging, and then I'm the one hissing in air between my teeth and closing my eyes.

Yup. That's it. Just close your eyes and pretend she's any other girl.

She leans down to kiss me and I decide to take my own advice. "Lift up," I say, grabbing her hips with both hands to urge her. She does, and then without any more prodding, she slips my cock between her legs and I slide in past her wetness.

"Oh, fuck," I moan. Because she feels so good. Her pussy is good and tight and when she sits back down in my lap she contracts her muscles around my shaft.

We pause for a moment, letting the lust take over. And then she begins moving. Up and down, then back and forth. I grip her ass, helping her, and then lean back a little so she can lean forward.

Her long hair brushes over my chest as she moves. Her forehead pressed against mine as she begins to breathe quicker and harder. Little moans escaping past her lips.

I could do this all night. I could do this forever.

But that kind of sex comes with feelings and we're not doing feelings tonight. So I say, "Hold on," as I grab her ass, scoot forward, and stand up—taking her with me.

"What are you doing?" She half laughs.

"Taking you into the dark," I say.

"Huh?"

But I don't answer her or explain what that means. Just carry her down the hallway to my bedroom, kick the door all the way open with my foot, and then place her on the bed.

My cock slips out, but that's OK. I reach back to the door, close it to hide the light from the living room, and then kneel on the bed, her body between my thighs, as I grab her ass and push her up towards the headboard.

She giggles, reaching for me, her fingertips finding the curve of my shoulder as I knee her legs open wider and slip my cock back inside her pussy.

She lifts her knees up until her calves are just below my shoulders so I can penetrate her deeper.

"Kali," I say, holding myself up with hands propped on the mattress. And then I lean down, my chest brushing against her breasts, and kiss her mouth.

This time I don't think. We don't fit perfectly. It's sloppy, and quick. With tongues twisting together and heavy breathing.

I thrust into her. Once, very hard, and she digs her fingernails into the skin of my biceps. When I pull back she grips me tighter, but my forward thrust is more demanding and deeper and this makes her gasp.

Fuck her till she comes. That's all this is.

So that's what I do. I start going faster. Harder. Until my hips are pounding hers and my balls are slapping against her ass.

"Yes," she moans. "Like that. I need it like that."

Which I refuse to hear, or think about, or read into… fuck it. We're fucking, that's all this is. One night of weakness—

"Aiden," she breathes. "Yes, Aiden. More. I need more."

I go faster, hammering her with more force then I've used during sex before. Scooting her up the bed until her head is pressed against the wooded headboard and the whole bed is moving with us. Creaking and squeaking as it hits the wall in perfect rhythm of my thrusting cock.

She threads her fingers into my hair, pulling my face down to hers, and we kiss. Or try to, but our momentum and motion is too much to maintain contact.

"Come," I tell her. "I need you to come."

"Slow down," she says, wiggling underneath me.

But I don't want to slow down. Slow means something else and that's not what this is. Lovemaking is slow. Fucking is fast.

But her legs wrap around my middle, squeezing me and preventing me from continuing my pounding.

"Yeah," she says, when I give in. "Like that."

'Like that' is… not fucking.

"Oh, God," she says. "You feel so damn good inside me. Do it just like that."

'Like that' is… slow, and careful, and perfect.

"Now kiss me, Aiden Edwards. Because I'm about to come all over your cock."

I don't want to kiss her. I know what'll happen if I kiss her. I will—

"Oh, hell, yes," she moans into my mouth. Because I'm already kissing her. And this time it's perfect, like it was before. This time it's real. It's a kiss like no other.

And even though I want this whole encounter to be meaningless and just another knee-jerk reaction at the end of a long, sad day… I can't quite talk myself into that. I can't quite make myself believe the lie.

Because it's not just that. It's not just fucking.

This is Kali fucking Anderson and I have liked her since the day we met.

She bucks her back, digging her nails so far into the skin behind my neck, I'm certain she's drawing blood. And she goes still, and stiff. Her mouth opens wide and I realize I'm still kissing her. But not just her mouth now, I'm kissing her neck. I'm nipping her earlobe, and the full weight of my body is pressed down on hers.

She moans, "God, yes," into my ear, sending that chill up my spine once again as her pussy becomes slick with her release.

I'm still fucking her slow. Didn't even realize it. Long, slow pushes combined with agonizing pull backs.

And then I'm there too.

I rise up, pulling out of her as I sit back on the bed. Hand reaching for my cock so I can pump the come out, aiming for her belly in the dark. But an instant later she's on her knees in front of me. Hand on my chest, pushing me backwards. She takes my cock right out of my hand and the next thing I know her lips seal around my throbbing, swollen head and suck.

"Oh, fuck," I groan.

Because that's it for me.

My come spills all over her tongue and slides down her throat.

CHAPTER EIGHT

I swallow him. All of it. And he moans, and groans, and fists my hair so he can hold me in place until he's finished. And then he lifts me off him, pushes me back onto the bed, and falls sideways on top of me.

"Shit," he says, out of breath and heart beating fast against mine. "Shit," he says again.

"Not what you expected?" I ask, curving my body into his as I close my eyes. His arm sneaks under my body and he holds me in a tight embrace.

"It was everything I expected," he mumbles.

Oh. Not what I was going for, but OK. But instead of saying that I say, "I just wanna sleep now."

He huffs out a breath that might be a smile mixed with a laugh. "Sure thing. No objections here."

I nuzzle my face into the crook of his neck as he reaches over, feeling for a blanket, and covers us up. The sudden warmth and closeness feels like protection and safety all at once and even though this day was one of the worst in my life, it ends better than it started.

"Good night, Kali," he murmurs, already drifting off.

"Night," I say back, suddenly wide awake. I can still feel the buzz from the whiskey but it's not enough to erase what just happened.

I just had sex with Aiden Edwards.

No. That's not what happened.

I just had sex with my brother's best friend.

Right after his funeral.

What kind of horrible sister am I? Why did I do this?

But of course, I know why.

I wanted to. And Kyle wasn't here to play interloper and stop us. For the first time in my life I was alone and Aiden was all mine.

I sigh and this makes Aiden shift position. A sudden urge to leave overtakes me. Just get my shit and walk out. But he's not sleeping that deep yet. If I move, I'll wake him up. Plus, I'm too drunk to drive all the way back to the city.

So I lie there. Forbidding myself from enjoying his loose embrace. Forbidding myself from replaying our first time over and over in my head.

Doesn't work.

I do enjoy him and I do replay it.

Especially the kisses. And the way he responded to me. And the way he nibbled my earlobe as I came. And the way he forced my head to stay in position as he came down my throat.

Then I get one of those irrational fears. Can Kyle see us? Is his spirit still hanging around? Did he just witness our ultimate betrayal?

I don't believe in ghosts, or God, or spirit realms, so I tell myself that's all nonsense.

Still, I can't get the image of Kyle out of my mind. I picture him pacing the room at the foot of the bed. Screaming at me. Screaming at Aiden. Taking a swing at him and unable to connect.

It's bad enough he's dead, but now we just went and made things worse.

I want to leave. I need to leave.

But I remain still.

I tell myself that I just need him to sleep deeper, then I'll get up and walk out.

But time passes. Hours pass and I'm still here.

Aiden has shifted position so many times he's now lying on his stomach, arms gripping the pillow under his face.

Light begins to seep in from the window and I can see his bedroom a little. It's small, just a bed and one nightstand off to the side. The curtains are sheer and blue. So is the comforter covering me.

But he's all the way on the other side of the bed now. There's no excuse for me to still be here. So I carefully—quietly—get up and walk into the living room. Put on all my clothes, grab my shoes, and leave the way I came in. Through the back, down the alley, and out onto the street.

My parents live about a mile and a half away and I walk the whole thing barefoot. It's early, barely six AM, and it's Saturday. Our sleepy little town isn't quite ready to wake up yet, so thankfully only a few cars pass as I walk.

When I get there I slip in the back door, find my purse, and then walk straight out to my car.

I know I should stay. Talk to my parents, at least. But I can't. I can't be here in this town without Kyle. And after what Aiden and I did, I don't think I could even look my parents in the eyes.

So I walk out to the guest parking area, get in my car, and drive two hours back to the city.

I'm just walking into my apartment when my phone buzzes an incoming text.

Aiden: Where'd you go?

I don't answer.

Just turn the phone off, take a shower, and climb into my bed.

When I wake up it's already late afternoon. And when the memory of what I did the night before comes rushing back, I dread looking at my phone.

But what I find waiting for me is both surprising and expected.

Three messages from my parents.

None, other than that first one, from Aiden.

Hmmm. I guess his regrets are as real as mine.

I make a cup of coffee real fast, then settle onto my couch and call my parents.

"There you are," my mother says, not even bothering with hello. "We're been calling you all day. Where are you?"

"Home," I say.

"Oh," my mother says. "We were expecting you at the reception last night."

"Right," I say, closing my eyes. Because I feel like I could sleep for another three days. "Aiden and I went to his place afterward. We stayed at the grave for a while, just talking. And then we went back to the garage and… got drunk, to be honest."

"Well, I'm just glad you're OK. We were worried about you."

"No, I'm OK," I say. Feeling anything but OK.

"Your father is still in bed," she says.

"Shit," I say. "I can come back. I'm supposed to work Sunday brunch tomorrow, but—"

"No," she says, cutting me off. "He'll be OK. It's just going to take time. People deal with grief in many ways. I'm up at the crack of dawn painting. That's what keeps me sane. But your father… well, he's dreading what comes next."

"What does come next?" I ask. Death is so foreign to me, I really have no clue what happens after a funeral.

"We have to clean out Kyle's house and then figure out what to do with it after the reading of the will."

"Right," I say, rubbing my temple. "The will. When is that again?"

"Friday afternoon. Here at Mr. Edwards's office."

"Shit," I say. "I didn't realize Mr. Edwards was handling this stuff."

"He is," my mom says. "Kyle and Aiden both made wills a few years ago when the business took off."

"Right," I say, still rubbing my temple. But the headache isn't responding to my massages. Hangover, I decide. "Of course they'd just use Aiden's dad."

"So you're coming for that?" my mother asks.

I want to say no. Very badly. But I skipped out on the reception and hearing that my dad isn't doing well—I decide I can't.

"For sure," I say. "I'll be there."

"Good." My mother sighs with relief. "How is Aiden?" she asks. "He was a mess the night before the funeral. Came over to our house and stayed the night on the couch."

"He did?"

"He was so upset. Did you two have a good talk?"

"Talk?" Jesus. I sound like an idiot today. "Yeah," I lie. "We did. It was a good… talk."

"Good," she says. Also on autopilot. I don't think I've ever had such a stinted, bumbling conversation with my mother before. "You know, most workplaces have bereavement time. You should use it, Kali. This is a huge change in your life. Losing a twin—"

"I know," I say, too sharply. "And I can't take time off." This is a lie. "We're down a chef at the restaurant and I have to fill in." Another lie. "Plus, it keeps my mind busy." Finally, some truth.

"OK, well." She sighs. "Rest up. You sound tired."

"I will, Mom. I love you."

She returns the sentiment and we hang up. I sit on my couch and just… do nothing. Forgetting about my coffee until it's cold and I have to get up and make another cup.

But now I'm lying to myself. Because I am thinking about something.

Not my dead twin, but Aiden.

His off-limits best friend who I had a one-night stand with last night.

CHAPTER NINE

I heard her leave. She tossed and turned so much last night, I woke up like sixteen times. And usually eleven shots in the span of ten minutes would be enough to sleep through the night, but it wasn't. I could've done a hundred shots and still been unable to sleep last night.

So I heard her leave. And there was this part of me that wanted to take her hand, pull her back into bed, and say, "It's OK, Kali. It's gonna be OK."

But the rational part of me couldn't tell the lie.

Nothing is OK. My best friend is dead. My business partner gone. And I fucked the one girl who was off limits right after his funeral.

I made the mandatory text a few hours after she left. I knew she'd either be sleeping in her childhood bedroom or at home in the city by that time.

Yup. It was the coward's way out but it was all I could manage.

She didn't even read it, so where she is now, I have no clue. The garage is closed on Saturday but I'm down there anyway, looking at the Jeep on the lift. Kyle's Jeep. The asshole Jeep that flipped and crushed him just four days ago.

I want to send this fucker to the junkyard.

No. I want to take a fucking ax to it and chop it up into little tiny pieces.

It's an old '78 CJ7 with a custom lift kit and thirty-nine-inch tires. Helluva good rock crawler. Even without fixing the body and suspension, I could sell this thing for almost fifteen grand. If I did fix it back up it'd fetch twenty-five, easy.

But I'm not gonna sell it. I'm either gonna destroy it or keep it forever.

I remember the day Kyle bought this Jeep. His mom and dad gave him five grand for his seventeenth birthday to get it. Kali was there because it was her birthday too and she also got a car, but one that wouldn't break down as she was driving it home off the used car lot. We were still kids back then. Still filled with wonder, and excitement. Our futures were bright and far away in our minds.

It was a piece-of-shit Jeep when Kyle bought it. Barely drivable. He broke down twice on the way home.

I smile, then laugh a little just thinking about it.

Kali rode with me and we followed Kyle and his new baby. That was the first time we'd been alone together in a while. Probably close to a year. I think Kyle knew I had a thing for her. He kept trying to get Kali to ride with him in the Jeep. It was her birthday too, he kept saying. She should ride in this spectacular monster he just purchased.

But it was drizzling that day and the Jeep didn't even come with a soft top. No doors, nothing. Just the roll cage. Kyle was soaked by the time he got it back to the townhouses but he didn't care.

Kali and I didn't care either. We spent almost an hour in my car alone, just talking. I didn't have a Jeep back then, just a reliable late-model Toyota Camry my parents gave me a few months back.

Kali was excited about senior year, I remember. We were all about making plans that summer. One year left and then what? I was always headed towards a tech school for auto mechanics and body work a few towns over. That crappy Jeep—this beautiful monster on the lift in front of me— was my school project the whole two years I was there.

I built the thing that killed my best friend.

I did that.

But Kali and I that day Kyle drove the beast home, we just talked. I didn't make a move on her. I knew better after that time I saw her naked. But I chatted her ear off. Asked her every question I could think of. It's been a long time since I had such a nice conversation with her.

I already knew I wanted her. I already knew that one day this would happen. I never suspected it'd take so long and I certainly never thought it would be Kyle's death that would spark it. Or this stupid Jeep, for that matter.

Such is life.

Kali said something to me that day that I never forgot though. She said, "Aiden, why don't you have a girlfriend? You're too handsome and sexy to not have a girlfriend."

And I said, "I'm saving myself for you, pretty thing."

She blushed so pink. Got so hot. She hid her face from me for a few minutes, just staring out the side window. And then she sighed and said, "Well. You're gonna have to kill Kyle if you want me all to yourself. Because he's the boss of us both."

I frown in the here and now. Thinking back on that day.

"I guess I did kill you after all," I say out loud. "Because I made you this death trap."

If I had an ax I'd kill it right now. Just hack it up into bits.

I don't.

I take my phone out instead and without even thinking, or questioning why I do it, I call Kali.

To my surprise, she picks up. "Hey," she says.

"How'd you know it was me?" I ask.

"Duh. I have your number in my phone."

"Hmmm. Didn't even know that. You've never once called me, ya know."

"Really?" she says.

"Really."

"Does that piss you off?"

"Nah," I say.

"So… do you need something?"

"Yeah," I say. "I think I need you."

"Aiden," she says.

"Not like that," I say. Lying. I do need her like that. But that response very clearly tells me she doesn't feel the same. "I just mean… the old us, you know? The friends us."

"I'm back in the city," she says.

"Oh," I say. "Yeah, I figured there was a good chance you ran away."

"I didn't run away."

"Then why didn't you wake me up? How did you even get back to your parents?"

"Walked. And I didn't wake you up because you were dead asleep."

"Right," I say.

There's an awkward silence after that. And then we both say the same thing at the same time. "We probably shouldn't have—"

We both stop.

Another pause and then I'm the one who continues. "We probably shouldn't have gotten drunk last night." Then add, just to be a dick, "That's what you were thinking too, right?"

She sighs. "Aiden, look. I had fun last night. Which comes with a whole lot of guilt all by itself. But we're not going to do this. It's disrespectful to my brother."

"OK," I say, feeling hot all of a sudden.

"He never wanted us to be together."

"Understood," I say.

"He'd be disappointed if he ever knew."

"Got it, Kali."

"Don't get pissed at me," she snaps. "I didn't ask for this."

"You kinda did," I say. "And you know what? I wasn't asleep when you left this morning. I was wide awake. And I let you go. So yeah, it was a mistake and I'm over it."

And then I end the call. It takes every ounce of self-control not to throw my phone at the wall. Instead, I just turn it off and toss it onto my tool cart.

Fuck her then, I decide. If Kali Anderson wants to fuck and forget, I'm happy to give her what she wants.

And besides, I think, looking up at the lift...

I've got a Jeep to kill.

CHAPTER TEN

"Of course I called him back." I'm saying this over dinner with my friend Alison. She doesn't know the history between Kyle, Aiden and me. We just became friends two years ago when I was going through my I'm-going-to-bake-dessert-for-money phase and she applied to be my assistant. Needless to say, the friendship outlasted the business.

"How many times?" Alison asks, shoving half a taco in her mouth. "Sorry," she says, wiping her mouth and chewing as she talks. "I skipped my snack today and I'm starving."

Snack. Sometimes I want to throttle her. She's one of those small, petite girls with perfect brown skin and dark curly hair that has natural honey-colored highlights in the sun. Going to the lake with her in a bikini is a lesson in humility.

"I know what you're thinking." She points at me. "And you know what my answer is?"

"Call him back again until he picks up?"

"Who? What? No, you're thinking about my taco and how I skipped a snack."

"I was not."

"Liar. Anyway, you're the one with the hips and tits. Good for you. I'm built like a boy so I get to stuff tacos in my mouth six times a day."

I laugh. "I'd rather have the tacos."

"Grass is always greener, honey. No one's ever satisfied."

"Anyway," I say.

"Anyway, yes. If you like him you just gotta spell it out, Kali. Men are… well, men."

"I don't know if I like him."

She shoots me one of those looks that says, *Bitch. Please.*

"OK, I like him." And then I sigh. "I've always liked him, Alison."

"How come this is the first I'm hearing about it? We're supposed to be each other's vault. And"—she points her finger at me again—"how did I not know you had a twin? Why are you living this double life?"

"I'm not," I say. Then frown.

"Sorry," Alison says. "Didn't mean to bring up your brother. I should've gone to the funeral with you. I'm a bad friend."

"No," I say. "You're an awesome friend. I just needed to do that myself."

"So tell me why you've been avoiding your brother for the past few years." Then she raises her eyebrows. "Oh. I see. It wasn't your brother you were avoiding, it was this Aiden guy."

I didn't plan this. I never meant to wander away from Kyle and Aiden the way I did. At least I don't think I did. It's just... "I have always liked him, Alison. Ever since I could remember. And he's always been off limits. Plus, you should see him. I mean, when we were kids he was just another cute boy but then when we turned sixteen he turned into this magnificent man with muscles and, holy hell, Ali. He's got tattoos now. And the business with Kyle—that's doing awesome. And he's always been a kind person. Always took care of me when I needed something. He's just... my one, you know? And I can't have him."

"The brother's best friend is tricky," she says. "I only have sisters so my big no-no was no dating the sisters' exes."

"Did you ever?" I ask.

She almost spits out her taco. "I have seven sisters, Kali. There's only so many men in the world."

"So you did?"

She nods. "Only once though." But then she actually puts down her taco and says, "But it was a mistake. My sister Ami didn't speak to me for almost a year. And at first I was like… well, I have six other sisters to drive crazy, I don't need her. But that guy was just using me to make her jealous and then…" She stops and waves her hand in front of her face like she needs to wipe that memory away. "Anyway, it was a mistake. Never did it again. But…"

"But what?"

She shrugs and eats the rest of her taco.

"I know what you're going to say. Or at least I know what you're thinking. You're thinking… Kyle is gone now, so—"

"I was not going to say that." Then she looks down at her plate. "But I was thinking it." She looks up at me again. "Don't you think he'd want you two to be happy?"

"He didn't want us to date when he was alive," I say, suddenly feeling sad. "Why would he change his mind now?"

She raises one eyebrow at me.

"I know he's dead," I say, feeling the ache of empty space in my heart. "But I want to respect his wishes."

"You don't know his wishes, Kali. You were avoiding him for years."

"Believe me, every time he had an inkling that Aiden and I were attracted to each other he made them very clear. I am not allowed to date his best friend and Aiden is not allowed to date his sister."

Alison frowns at me. One of those big, pouty frowns. "I'm sorry, sweets. It's hard, I know. But you only get one life and no one understands better than Kyle right now. I didn't know him, and I wish I had. Because you're amazing so I know he was amazing too. But I promise you, Kali. I swear on my heart. He'd have wanted you to be happy."

"Maybe," I say.

"Keep calling Aiden. Bug him until he can't ignore you anymore. Say what's in your heart and leave it at that. If he feels the same, great. You can each have a spiritual heart-to-heart with Kyle and come to an understanding. And if he doesn't, then it's better to know than spend the rest of your life wondering 'what if.'"

She's right. "You're right," I say.

"Give me your phone."

"Why?"

She smirks at me. "You know why."

I laugh and I'm not even drunk. It feels good to laugh after the sadness and despair of the past several days.

"Come on," she says, holding out her hand and wiggling her fingers. "Hand it over."

"You're gonna—"

"It's just a text, I promise."

I grumble, but reach into my purse and get my phone, handing it over with equal parts hesitation and relief. Alison is one of those people who just says what's on her mind. No matter what. And while some of our friends find that annoying, I think it's amazing. I wish I had her nerve and guts.

"Be nice though," I say. "He's hurting too."

"I can be nice," she says, then sends me a wicked grin as she scrolls through my contacts and starts typing. "There," she says, handing it back.

I'm afraid to glance down at the screen. "Alison!"

"What?"

"'I'm going cut off your balls and serve them for dinner if you don't answer my calls?'"

"It's pithy and descriptive. No room for misinterpretation. Now press send."

I make a face.

"Do it."

And because I love her, and because she's better at this confrontation thing that I could ever hope to be, and (mostly) because I just want to hear Aiden's voice—I do it. I press send.

"There," she says, brushing taco crumbs off her mouth. "It's done. If he doesn't call you back, you'll know it's better to move on."

I spend the next few minutes glancing down at my screen while Alison talks about her new idea for a bakery. "We already tried this," I say, just as she's getting started.

"We did it wrong," she says. "This idea is good."

So I do my best to get lost in her dream because it's my dream too. I don't want to cook steaks and pasta for the rest of my life. I got into cooking for the treats. It's just so hard to make it on baking alone.

By the time we're hugging goodbye Aiden still hasn't called me back. I walk home from the taco place, phone in hand. Willing it to ring, or ding a text, or run out of battery so I can pretend he tried to make contact and couldn't.

Doesn't work.

My battery is fine, there are no texts, and no missed calls either. So I didn't magically pass through a dead zone during the three-block walk from dinner.

My body is tired, my mind is exhausted, and my emotions are all out of whack.

And I'm sad. I miss my brother. I miss my twin. I don't even know how to define myself anymore. And this self-pity feels over-indulgent because no one in my current city life even knows about my old small-town one.

I lie down in bed, not even bothering to get undressed. And even though I think I'll never sleep again, I do. I sleep.

When I wake up the next morning I feel refreshed and happy for exactly two seconds. Because that's how long it takes my brain to say, *Kyle is dead and Aiden's not speaking to you.*

Work, I decide.

I go to work and hope this misery won't get worse before it gets better.

I work on the Jeep for sixteen hours straight, pulling off the fenders and the grill, the wheels and tires. Hell, I even pull out the seats. Kyle and I have been working on this Jeep since he was seventeen years old. This was how we knew we wanted to open a business together. This was our passion, our life, our connection.

And all of that feels empty now.

I go up to bed at four in the morning on Sunday. But sleep is fitful and unproductive, so I find myself back down in the garage before noon. Still ripping shit apart.

The next thing I know the guys are arriving for work on Monday and I don't know where my weekend went. All I know is that the Jeep is in pieces and that makes me happy for some reason.

They were all at the funeral on Friday. Probably went to the reception afterward too. Hell, probably wondered why I didn't.

But they're quiet when they come in and see me working. Unable to meet my gaze, unwilling to start a conversation. Kyle has been my best friend my whole life. It's always been us against them.

Not these guys. They're all friends too. But Kyle was the only one I really hung out with. The only one who mattered. And seeing Kali after all these years of her being distant has brought back all the old times when we were a trio.

My heart just hurts thinking about when we were kids.

I knew we shouldn't have had sex after the funeral. I knew Kyle would not approve and I feel like such a goddamned disappointment to him right now.

"Hey, Aiden?"

I look up from my tool cart and see Clyde, my paint guy, standing next to me. Then realize I've been staring down at my tools for so long, I don't even know how long he's been standing there.

"Yeah," I say, my voice raw and rough. I clear it then say, "What's up, Clyde?"

"I just want you to know…" He stops. And I realize his eyes are watering.

"Don't, dude," I whisper. "I can't right now."

He puts up a hand and nods his head. "Sure," he says. "I know. But we're here for you, OK? And if you need more time, just… take it. OK? We'll handle things."

I look over my shoulder and see all the other guys looking back at me. Jessie is holding a socket wrench in his hand, twirling the end over and over again so it makes that ratcheting sound. Len is pouring a cup of coffee and it spills over the side of his cup because he's not paying attention. And Gary is sitting in a chair by my office, elbows on knees, head in hands, looking up at me through his too-long hair.

Clyde grips my shoulder and says, "Go sleep, Aiden. You look like you need it." I nod my head, barely understanding as Clyde takes a wrench out of my hand and places it neatly in the spot where it belongs on my cart. "We got this."

I nod, then notice my phone peeking out from under a rag on my cart. I turned it off on Saturday morning and haven't thought about it since.

Kali's face comes to mind. The argument we had. And then I feel guilty for not calling her back.

I pick it up, slip it into my back pocket, and turn to Clyde. "I think I'll take you guys up on that offer." And then I walk down the hallway to my apartment on autopilot.

Upstairs feels lonely even though I've been living here by myself for more than ten years. Everyone comes up here to eat lunch. Kyle and I would spend hours up here when the work was slow. Just kickin' it, watching sports, or movies. Talking about Jeeps and the crawler competitions coming up.

Thinking about that makes me remember that we've got four or five of them scheduled over the next several months. We usually do them together but this one he was at last week was some private club thing he just got involved in. I stayed behind to work because he said he wasn't gonna do anything but hang out. He said he just needed a day off in the rocks.

Why didn't I fucking go with him?

I slump down on the couch and remember my phone again. Pull it out, power it on, and find twenty-six notifications. Texts and missed calls from pretty much everyone I know. Including all the guys downstairs.

But Kali's are the ones I look at first. Lots of voicemails. "Call me," she says. Then that last text on Saturday night. *I'm going to cut off your balls and serve them for dinner if you don't answer my calls.*

I laugh. "Jesus, Kali. What the fuck?" But I find her contact in my phone and call.

"You," she says, answering my call without a hello. "I'm mad at you."

"I'm sorry," I say.

"You hung up and ghosted on me."

"I'm sorry," I say again.

"I don't want you to be sorry," she says. And I can hear the strain in her voice. The sadness. "I just want you to pick up your fucking phone when I call, is that too much to ask?"

"I'm—"

"Stop it," she says. "I'm the one who's sorry, OK?"

I make a face. "Why are you sorry?"

She huffs. "For being a bitch, OK? I was a bitch. It's just…" She sighs. "I've had this crush on you since I was eight and I didn't sleep with you on Friday because I was drunk, all right? I did it because I wanted to."

I smile. And it feels so good, and so foreign, I think I forgot what smiling was. That's dumb because one week ago Kyle and I were fucking with Gary because he needs a haircut and our insults were so spectacular I thought I was gonna piss my pants laughing.

"Are you there?" Kali asks.

"I'm here." I sigh. "Just… not really here, if you know what I mean."

"I do," she whispers. "It's got to be hard to go down to the shop and not see him there."

"It is," I say. Because it really is. "Is everything OK?"

"No." She sighs. "It's not."

"Yeah, I get it."

"But I wanted to see if we could meet up for lunch on Friday before the reading of the will."

"Shit," I say. "I forgot about that."

"We could skip it," she offers.

But we can't. Not after we skipped the reception. People forgive you on funeral day. You get a pass for being selfish and self-absorbed. But they expect you to pick yourself up and move on and that includes showing up for the will reading when your business partner dies.

"No, we should go."

"Yeah," she agrees. "We should."

"So yeah," I say. "I'd love to have lunch. Wanna meet me here on Friday?"

"What time?"

"Kali," I say. "Any time. There is no time when it comes to you. This place is yours as much as it is mine."

"I'm not sorry," she says.

"I'm not either," I say back.

"See you Friday, then?"

"See ya Friday."

We hang up and as soon as I throw my phone down on the couch I have an urge to call her back. Tell her how I really feel. Tell her all the things I never could.

But Kyle is in my head warning me. Warning me to stay the fuck away from his sister.

So I just slump over and go to sleep instead.

The rest of the week pretty much goes just like that. Sleep until some weird hour—usually about the time the guys downstairs are going home. Then get up, shower, microwave a burrito and eat it on the way down to the shop. Make coffee out of habit, even though it's evening and not morning. Then work on tearing the Jeep down. By Thursday night it's pretty much a skeleton with an engine and I realize I have nothing left to rip apart.

But I don't want to stay up all night thinking about it because Kali will be here tomorrow and I don't want her to see me looking like a walking, talking, sleep-deprived maniac.

So I take a sleeping pill. It's an old bottle, well past the expiration date, but I take two to make up for that and then jump in the shower to wash the day's car filth off me, and climb into bed.

I wake up mid-morning to the sound of the compressor downstairs as the guys work on… whatever the fuck they're working on. I don't even know what jobs we have going right now.

But it's finally Friday and Kali will be here soon. Since it's the reading of the will I need to clean up for real. So I shave for the first time in a week and then realize I only own one suit and it's still on the floor of my living room from when Kali and I had sex.

So… no suit today. I put on a pair of newish dark jeans, a brown button-down shirt, and my good brown boots that don't have oil stains and metal flakes all over them. Then I look in the bathroom mirror, run my fingers through my hair, and tell myself it's gonna be OK.

Which is funny, in an ironic way. Because I said that last Friday too. But I think I really believed it last week and this week I don't. I thought painful things got better with time? Maybe there's some in-between stage I never knew about? The stage when things get worse and worse before they get better.

Rock bottom, I guess they call that.

I don't want Kali to be my rock bottom. I really don't.

"Knock-knock," she calls from the living room. "You here, Aiden?"

"Yeah," I say, turning away from the mirror, then flicking the bathroom light off as I exit into the hallway.

And then I see her. Kali. Standing in my front room, wearing cream-colored wide-legged linen slacks and a matching button-down blouse tucked in with a gold belt. Her dark hair is shiny and smooth, falling in waves over her shoulders like a waterfall.

She looks like... summer. And that reminds me of all the summers we spent together growing up. Just her, and me, and Kyle. Building forts in the woods or just wandering around like wild animals. Except Kali was always wearing a dress. Something summer-y and usually white. With flowers on it, or maybe polka dots. I was forever worried she was gonna get dirty because she was such a pretty thing. And Kyle and I were always in jeans or shorts. And our t-shirts always had mud stains or food stains on them.

Still, Kali was pretty. And she always knew who was growing strawberries in their garden every summer. She always had a plan for stealing the forbidden fruit.

God, I love her.

"You look pretty today," I say, walking into the living room, suddenly unsure what to say or do.

She looks down at her outfit, then up at me. "Thanks. You look nice too. How was your week?"

"My week?" I sorta laugh. "My week was spent dismantling Kyle's Jeep."

She nods, pressing her lips together. "I thought that was his Jeep up on your lift. But I wasn't sure. It's nothing but a frame."

"Yeah," I say, running my fingers through my hair again.

"What are you doing to it?"

"Killing it," I say.

"Oh." Then she makes a noise that could be a laugh or maybe just a huff of frustration.

"You wanna go to the sandwich shop?" I ask her, trying to change the subject. "For lunch?"

"Oh, God. The sandwich shop. I don't even remember the last time I ate there. I can't believe that place is still in business."

"It's not," I say. "Well, it is. But it's changed hands a few times over the years and for whatever reason, every time it gets sold the new owners never change it. Same menu, same tables and chairs, same bad country music."

She laughs. "Sounds perfect."

And it kinda is. Because it's right next door to my father's law office.

I grab my wallet off the small dining table, shove it in my back pocket, then pick up my keys and walk over to the door, holding it open for her. "After you," I say.

Kali smiles at me and walks through.

Downstairs all the guys stop working to look at us. Clyde says, "Later, Kali."

"Bye, Clyde."

He's the only one who really knows her. Been working with us since the very beginning. The other guys came along during her self-imposed hiatus from the Aiden, Kyle, and Kali show. So they just watch us leave.

"Wanna walk?" I ask her, once we're outside. "Or drive?"

"Walk," she says. Then she takes my hand.

I look down at it for a moment and she lets go. But I grab it again and say, "No. I like that."

We look at each other for a few moments, but I look away first. The town is small, but it's lunchtime. So there's people around. The beeping of a truck as it backs up to the building next door. A couple of old guys shouting to each other across the main street about mis-delivered mail, and another old guy riding his horse up to the pizza and beer place.

I don't know that guy's name, but every day, without fail, he shows up in town on his horse, ties it to a tree, and then goes inside.

"What the hell?" Kali laughs, looking at the guy and the horse.

"Don't ask. I have no clue. Personally, I think he's some old drunk who lost his license and that's his only option for getting to and from the bar."

"Does Mrs. Frett still walk her ponies around town?"

"Every fucking morning I find pony shit on the sidewalk. So, yeah. She does."

"This town." Kali chuckles. "I'd forgotten how weird it was."

"See what you've been missing out on?" I say, giving her hand a squeeze. "That city of yours has nothing on us."

"True," she says. "Do you get out my way much, Aiden?"

I glance at her, find her looking at me, then shake my head. "No reason, I guess."

She presses her lips together and nods. "Yeah. Kyle didn't either. I wish I hadn't wasted all these years with him."

I don't know what to say to that, so I say nothing. I'm not good at this kind of shit. I don't know how to say the right thing to make people feel better or comfort them. I guess that's why we ended up having sex last week.

I want to be better than that. I want to tell Kali all the things I feel about her. Especially all the things I feel about last weekend. I just don't know how. I can't quite come up with the right words, or sentiment, or expression to let her know she's important. That we are important and that… yeah, Kyle is gone but we're still here.

And even if I did know how to spit all that out… what does it mean, anyway?

Does it mean we should get together for real?

I don't know.

So I say nothing.

I don't know why I reached for his hand. I just did. And the second it happened, and the one that came next when he just kinda looked at it, I regretted it.

But then that instinctive action turned into something nice. So no regrets about that. But… I do have regrets about everything else. Not that I'd like to take back having sex with him last weekend because I don't. I just wish we could find a way past this uncertainty and move forward.

And then I don't know what moving forward looks like… so I give up trying to figure things out.

"I miss this town," I say. Because we're both being too quiet. Then add, "I'm going to make it my mission to come home as often as possible."

I hesitantly look over at Aiden from the corner of my eye, trying to get a glimpse of his response, but he appears deep in thought.

Then we're at the sandwich shop and Aiden opens the door for me, waving me forward. When did he get these manners? I feel like we're strangers these days. My impression of him is still one left over from us being kids. When he used to tease me and drive me crazy. When he was all boyish charm and playful antics.

And now he's so much more than that. He's got style, for one thing. He looked fantastic in that suit last week and today, this kinda business-casual style—it's flattering on him. Especially when his regular clothes are usually just old jeans and t-shirts.

We enter the shop, order our sandwiches—he gets a Philly steak and I get a turkey on wheat (some things never change)—and then take our number and find a table in the back.

"So what's going on in your world, Kali? You know what my life is like. Pretty much the same as always. But what do you do out there in the world?"

"Cook," I say. "I'm at a fancy steak and pasta place now."

"Do you like it?"

I shrug. "I guess. It pays what I need. I'm head chef there, so that's nice. But is this what I envisioned when I went to chef's school? No. I wanted to bake."

"So why don't you bake?"

I sigh. "There's corporate baking—like bread companies and stuff like that—and then there's mom-and-pop bakeries. Or trendy startups. Corporate baking isn't really baking in my eyes. So that would kill my soul. And I can't make a living at a mom-and-pop bakery."

"So start your own trendy place," he says.

"I tried," I say. "It didn't really get off the ground."

"Why not?" he asks, reaching across the table to take both my hands in his.

Our eyes meet. His are mesmerizing. Light blue-green that contrast with his darker hair and just… draw you in. Make you want to get lost in them.

He starts to let go of my hands, but I squeeze him back. Letting him know I like it. "I dunno," I say, answering his last question. "Bad planning? Bad timing? It's expensive to rent space in the city. You have to be somewhere where there's traffic and those places come with high price tags. So…" I shrug. "Not enough capital, I guess."

"Ah," he says. "This town doesn't have a bakery. We could use one if you ask me."

"Are you trying to get me to move back home?" I ask, unable to stop the smile spreading across my face.

"Maybe," he says. "It's not the worst place in the world to live."

"No, it's not. I love this town. We had a great childhood here, right?"

He nods. "Yeah." Then frowns. "We really did." Then he lets go of my hands and leans back in his chair. "I don't know what life looks like without Kyle, Kali. I can't even begin to picture it. I feel… alone, ya know?"

I nod my head as my eyes begin to water. "I know. But you're not alone, you have me."

He stares at me for a few moments. "Not really though. You're two hours away. We never see each other. And even if we did try to make this work—if you ever wanted, that is—two hours is close and far at the same time."

I nod and realize my throat is tightening up like I want to cry. "I do," I say. "Two stupid hours is a lifetime when you're working all the time and that traffic seems insurmountable when all you want to do is go home and sleep."

He opens his mouth to say something, but the counter person calls out our number and he just sighs instead. Then gets up, grabs our sandwich baskets and some napkins, and returns to the table, passing me my food.

We eat in silence for a little bit. Mostly people watching as locals come in in work clothes to grab a bite. And by the time we're done, it's almost time to walk over to his father's office for the reading of the will.

Aiden cleans up our table, throws everything in the trash, and then takes my hand.

I swing them a little. Like we're kids again. And then I have an overwhelming desire to be that kid again. Run around the woods with him and Kyle and just be wild. Steal strawberries out of people's gardens and climb apple trees.

"I've missed you," he says, stopping in front of his father's little house on Main Street that acts as an office. He can't look me in the eyes for a moment, but then he draws in a breath and manages. "I've really, really missed you. And I have this whole time. It's not Kyle's death that's making me miss you, Kal. It's just… that's just how I feel."

I frown and nod. "I've missed you too and—"

But then we're interrupted by his father poking his head out the door. "Coming inside?" he asks.

Aiden looks at him for a second, then tugs on my hand and says, "Yeah, we're coming."

My parents are already here, sitting in the conference room holding hands. They look down at our hands, and Aiden and I both instinctively pull apart. Like we were just caught doing something wrong.

My mother smiles at me and motions to the chair next to her. The conference room is small and so is the table, so Aiden takes the seat across from me, next to my father.

Aiden and I trade an apprehensive stare and then his father begins.

In the end, it's mostly what we expect. Aiden gets the shop, I get Kyle's Jeep and a bunch of stuff from when we were kids, and my parents get his little house a few blocks over. But we also each get something else.

"A phone number?" my father asks.

"It's some kind of app," Aiden's dad says. "Called Dead Notes. I know, terrible name. But Kyle thought it was cool."

Aiden huffs out a laugh. "He would."

"What is it?" my mom asks.

"You leave a message for your loved ones and it's connected to a phone number. They can call it whenever they want and hear your voice. So Kyle made one for each of you." He passes us each an envelope. "It's in there."

"What do they say?" I ask.

"I don't know, Kali," Mr. Edwards says. "He didn't share that with me."

All five of us just kinda look at each other, and then Mr. Edwards is saying, "Well, that's it. Anyone have any objections? Or questions?"

"Nope," I say. And everyone echoes the same.

Mr. Edwards stands up, which is our cue to also stand, which we do. And then everything gets awkward.

Because now what? That's it, I guess. The funeral is over, the will has been read, and Kyle is officially gone, so there's nothing left to do.

"Do you want to come back to the house?" my mom asks.

"No," I say, shaking my head. "I just want to go for a walk, if that's OK?"

My parents each kiss me on the cheek and we promise to get together soon.

It's what we do and say every time. And every time it's a lie. Because I just go home and do my thing.

A few minutes later Aiden and I are walking in the general direction of the shop, my parents are on their way home, and Aiden's dad is presumably back to work.

"So…" Aiden says. "I guess I owe you an apology."

"For what?"

"Your Jeep."

"Oh," I say, chuckling. "Well… whatever you want to do with it, is fine with me."

"Yeah." He sighs. "OK." But then he stops and takes both my hands in his. "I don't know why this is so hard to say, it just is. But I feel like this could be my last chance, you know? So I have to say it." He takes another deep breath and then, on the exhale, he says, "I don't want you to leave. Don't leave, Kali. Don't go home tonight. Just stay with me."

Everything about this moment is honest. The way he struggles to put his feelings into words. The way his words make me feel as he says them. The seemingly endless, awkward moment of silence as he waits for my answer. And I wish I could say what he wants to hear, but I can't.

Still, there is another option.

"I have to work brunch tomorrow. It's the weekend and we open at ten. So I have to be there early." His face, his expression—it's so sad I want to kiss him right here, right now. In the middle of town. "You can come home with me though," I say, offering up my alternative option. "If you want to, that is. You could stay the weekend with me, Aiden. I'll be home by four tomorrow and then—"

"Yes," he says, pulling me into a hug. "Yes. I'd love that."

I hug him back. And for the first time since learning of Kyle's death I feel… OK. Maybe not good, but OK is better than filled with despair and sadness.

CHAPTER THIRTEEN

We take her car and ride into the city together. I like that idea because it basically means she's stuck with me for the weekend. And even if we do get into another fight—which I don't think we will, but just in case—she will have to spend another two hours with me to drive me home. And then think about her actions for another two hours when she drives back.

I smile at that just thinking about it. Call that plotting, or scheming if you want. But I call it strategy.

"What are you smiling about?" Kali asks, just as we pull into the parking garage for her building.

"You," I say, slowly turning my head to look at her.

"Should I ask?"

"Nah," I say. "Just feel good about it."

She chuckles. Then pulls her car into her spot.

We get out, I grab my backpack with a change of clothes, and ride the elevator up to her floor—seven—thinking about how things might change after this weekend as we walk down the hallway in silence.

"I think I'm nervous," she says, putting her key in her door.

"Why?"

"Because… this is me. And you don't know me anymore."

"What? You got a creepy doll collection in there or something? Doing witchcraft in your spare time? Oh, I know what it is. You're afraid I'll find all your sex toys."

"You're dumb," she says, swinging the door open.

I walk forward at her urging but then say, over my shoulder, "But you do have sex toys, right?"

"No comment," she says, closing the door behind her.

I walk down the short hallway and stop in her living room. Trying to get a sense of who she is now. Because she's right. I've pretty much stayed the same all these years. Still live in my home town. Still do the same job. Same friends, same general style of clothes, same hobbies, same everything.

But Kali is a mystery and this is my first step towards unraveling all her secrets.

Her place is homey. Cozy, they call it on those TV shows when no one wants to admit the place is kinda small. It's not tiny or anything, but it's not big, either. Definitely not her dream home, I will say that.

At least I don't think it is. I could be wrong, I barely know her anymore. But no one aspires to living in a one-bedroom apartment in a nondescript part of the city. It's good. It's fine, but that's it.

Her color scheme is neutral, which surprises me a little. Just because she was never a neutral girl when we were younger. Always wearing girly things. Dresses, and hairbands, and ribbons. So for some reason I expected her place to look like one of those farmhouse decorating shows. Pinks, and light blues, and couches with feminine patterns on them.

But her couch is taupe, and her walls are a similar shade that leans towards gray. Her end tables are stainless steel and her dining table isn't round, but square. And I don't know why it feels off, but it does. Maybe because my dining table is round and her family's dining table was always round so I expected her to be like us.

"You don't like it," she says. I realize she's been watching me take in her place.

"I like it," I say. "It's nice. Very… city."

"And I'm not," she says, dropping her keys into a small glass dish by the door.

"You're not," I say, being serious. "You're still that pretty little girl who wore summer dresses and pigtails with ribbons. You're still that same girl with the light blue bedroom who had framed flowers on her walls. You're the girl who helped make forts in the woods and climbed trees like a monkey."

"Is that how you think of me? As her?"

"You are her," I say. "So yeah."

"I guess I am," she says. "I still feel like her. Sometimes. But then I get dressed, and go out into the city, and I'm someone else." She shrugs. "You know, I don't think I know who I am anymore. I think I've felt this way for a long time and Kyle's death just made it all real."

I don't want to agree with her, so I don't. But there's a part of me that agrees with her. Who is this woman who lives here? Who owns non-descript furniture and paints her walls taupe? Who is *this* Kali?

I'm not complaining. I don't wish she were someone else. Or some*thing* else, either. I just don't know her anymore.

So I get what she's saying and how Kyle's death has her questioning everything. Every choice she's made since she went one way and Kyle and I went another.

"I know," I say, walking over to her and pulling her into a hug. "He was you, and you were him. He wasn't my twin but I feel that way as well. I miss him. So much. I don't even think I realized how much until the guys showed up for work on Monday. That's when it hit me that everything was now… different. And it was never going back to the way it was."

She sucks in a deep breath of air and pulls back a little. Not a lot, like she's hinting she wants me to let go of her. Just enough so she can look me in the eyes. Then she says, "I actually do have sex toys."

Which makes me laugh out loud. "Is that right?"

"Mmm-hmmm." And then she leans in and kisses me. Just a little fluttering kiss on my lips. No tongue. Just… nice.

But of course, I take it to the next level. Seeing her today, after what happened last week, just made me want her more. Made me wish I didn't waste seven whole days ignoring her.

So I bring my hands up to her head, hold her there, and kiss her harder. Open-mouthed with tongue. She kisses me back as her fingertips grab on to my shirt, fisting it in her hands.

I pull back first and say, "Is this all it is?"

"No," she says too quickly. "I like you, Aiden. I've always liked you."

"And so… we're going to have a repeat of last week? Sex, then regrets, then fight?"

"I told you, I'm not sorry. I don't have regrets."

"But you're not certain either, are you?"

"Are you?" she asks.

"No," I say. "I'm not. But I want to be here with you. I want to stay all weekend and eventually meet your friends. See you work and get to know you again."

"Oh, God," she says, smiling. "You want to meet Alison?"

"Who's Alison?" It bothers me that I have to ask. I should know her friends. I suddenly miss the Kali I never got to know. And knowing her now isn't quite the same thing. I feel like I lost time with her.

It's not her fault we drifted apart. It's not really my fault either. It just… is. That's all. Just is what it is.

"Well, Alison," Kali says. "She's… a lot of girl. A *lot* of girl." Kali laughs. "That's all."

"Mmm," I say, kissing her again. "So are you. So now I know why you two are friends."

"You want to know me, then?" she says.

"Yeah, I do. Let's start with your sex toys. Because every woman in her thirties has accumulated a nice collection of sex toys."

"Maybe I only have one?" she asks. "And maybe it's broken and old because I never need to use it."

"Hmmm," I say, practically growling.

"Kidding."

"So where do you keep them?" I ask, pulling away and walking down the hall to her bedroom.

"Where are you going?"

"To find them," I say. "Duh."

She laughs, then comes after me, pulling on my arm. "You're not serious."

"Fuck yeah, I am. I bet they're in your nightstand."

"Is that where your other girlfriends keep them?" she asks, winking.

"If I had a girlfriend, believe me, she'd be like you. She wouldn't need them. I'd make sure she was all set before her day even started."

"Oh," Kali says. "Well, then. I guess you don't need to go looking, do you?"

"Nice try," I say, grinning as I pull away from her grip and go into her bedroom. "Nightstand," I say, pulling out the drawer.

"Nope," she says.

"Jesus, Kali. This drawer is a mess of… why do you keep your passport in your nightstand?" I ask, holding it up.

"OK," she says, putting up her hands. "Confession time. I'm as sloppy on the inside as I am neat on the outside. Every drawer is a junk drawer."

A memory of me poking around her room once when we were kids comes back to me. We were like, I dunno, ten or eleven, maybe. And all three of us were in Kali's room for some reason. Plotting some woodland adventure, maybe. And I opened her desk drawer and found everything you can imagine. Glue, a diary, pens and markers, paints, an old letter to Santa Claus, a dog collar, even though they didn't have a dog. A few packets of sunflower seeds—not the kind you eat, but the kind you plant. Headbands, nail polish, a million stray bits of paper. A sock. Just one. Lots of costume jewelry and photos.

This drawer is exactly that, only the grown-up version.

She pushes it closed before I can start picking up one of her many random receipts. "The toys?" she says, like it's a question and I have the answer.

"Right," I say. "That's where we were before I realized you're a secret hoarder. So where are they?" I waggle my eyebrows at her. Amused, and excited, and maybe even a little intimidated that I'm actually here in her apartment.

"Bathroom," she says.

"Bathroom? How the hell do you whip out a toy during sex when it's all the way across the hall in the bathroom?"

"Wait," she says, holding up a hand and laughing. "You use them *during* sex?"

"You don't?" I ask. And then I laugh and walk into the bathroom, pulling open her drawer of makeup, then opening her cupboard to find—"Bingo," I say, pulling out the basket. "Nice collection, by the way." I hold up a blindfold with a questioning look. "Who uses this on you?"

"It's a sleep mask," she says.

"Liar," I say, shoving it in my pocket. "So you've never used… this"—I hold up a lime-green vibrator—"during sex?'"

"Do people do that? Use toys with other people?"

"What?" I laugh. Like loud. "It's like the whole point."

"No, the whole point is to have an orgasm when you're in a dry spell."

"Oh, Kali," I say, unable to stop my laugh. "You're not serious, right?"

"What do *you* do with them?"

"I…" I want to say, *What don't I do with them?* But that sounds like I'm a man whore. "How about I show you?" I say instead. And before I can remind myself this is my best friend's sister and I'm not gonna pull out the Aiden Edwards man-whore moves on her, I push her up against the bathroom wall and turn the vibrator on.

"What are you doing?" she laughs, shoving me away with two hands on my chest.

I decide not to give in. I decide not to think at all and just... do something I'd do. She showed me the real her today, I can at least return the favor. So I don't let her push me away, I just lower the vibrator—which appears to have a full charge because it's humming loudly—and place it between her legs.

She squirms, crossing her legs so I can't have access. Then she says, "You have to take my clothes off first."

"Do I?"

She laughs again. "You're gonna get my pants all wet."

"No, Miss Anderson. *You're* going to get your pants all wet. And you're gonna like it too." I press my chest up again her breasts and make sure the vibrator is in just the right place. "Just relax," I say. Because it's clear she's not been introduced to the kinky side of sex before. That blindfold probably *is* a sleep mask. "I got this, Kal."

She lets out a nervous laugh.

"I came in your mouth last week," I say. "Trust me, this is gonna be easy."

"Oh, my God," she says.

"What's up?" I say. "You were all dirty-talking me last time."

"Did I?" she says. "Oh, shit. I did. I was drunk. And sad. I'm not drunk. Maybe we should get drunk?"

"Nice offer," I muse. But the real takeaway from her statement was that she's not sad. She didn't say it, but she implied it. And I realize I'm not sad either. I'm actually feeling better now that we're here at her place and the memories of Kyle aren't all around me. "We're not getting drunk. We're doing this sober. So just… relax, OK? I promise, I really do got this."

She sucks in a deep breath of air and lets it out. Eyes locked on mine as she nods.

I lean in to her a little more, kissing her neck as I move the vibrator between her legs. "If it's not in the right spot," I whisper into her ear, "put it where you like it."

She exhales, like this makes her nervous. But her hand reaches down to mine and a moment later she's repositioning the vibrator so it's directly over her clit.

"Right there?" I ask, turning my head so I can see her face. Her eyes are closed and her mouth is open just a little, her tongue touching the tip of her teeth in a way that looks both seductive and sweet at the same time.

"Yes," she says, her hand reaching for my cock.

I'm nearly hard as it is, but when she grips me through my jeans the blood rushes in and fills me up.

I grind against the pressure of her hand. Wanting more. I figured we'd have sex this weekend. Eventually. Didn't plan on getting her so hot right away, but fuck it.

I've missed out on years of Kali Anderson and that ends right now.

CHAPTER FOURTEEN

His cock is thick and hard under his pants and all I want is to take it out and feel it in my palm. Press my thumb over his tip and tease him until he's wet too. I'm no stranger to sex but he makes me nervous. This is Aiden Edwards. *My* Aiden Edwards. And I know we've already done this, but that was different. That was drunk, after-funeral sex and this is sound-mind-and-body sex.

So all these thoughts about what happens next start swirling up in my brain. All the what ifs that come with living two hours apart. All the doubts about Kyle, and the future—

"Shhhh," Aiden whispers in my ear. "Whatever you're thinking about, just let it go."

"I'm not," I whisper back, lying.

"I can tell, Kali. I've known you almost thirty years." And then he nips my earlobe.

Which sends chills through my whole body and makes me shrug my shoulders so he'll ease up.

"How about we go do this somewhere else? Huh?" He takes the vibrator away from me and pushes, ever so slightly, on the small of my back.

"Sure," I say, leading him across the hall to the bedroom. But once we're there, standing at the foot of the bed, tingly apprehension floods my body. I'm holding my breath, looking at my feet when the tip of his finger touches the bottom of my chin.

I look up and meet his gaze.

"I've always loved you. I just need to say that right now. It's always been you in my fantasies, Kali. I can't even count the number of times I fell asleep thinking about you or the number of happily-ever-after daydreams I had for us."

"Did it look like this?" I ask, still anxious.

"No," he says. "Well, yeah," he amends, then laughs a little. "I did all kinds of dirty things to you in some of them. But mostly they were about being with you. I want to be with you." He pauses. "Do you want to be with me?"

"Always," I say. "I've always wanted you."

He reaches his hand towards my face, brushing his knuckles down my cheek, then my neck, pausing at the top of my breast. He grins. Wickedly. Like a man about to undress me. And then he does.

One button at a time is popped open on my blouse until he reaches the waistband of my slacks and has to pull my shirt out to finish. Then he opens up my shirt and places his hands over my breasts, squeezing softly.

I stare up at his face the entire time. Wanting to memorize it. Wanting to witness every expression and emotion as he does all this.

"Now me," he says, taking my hands and bringing them up to the collar of his shirt. I think I hold my breath as I unbutton each button and pull his shirt out of his jeans. When I open him up the first thing I see is the tattoos covering his heart. They're words. I knew this. I saw him last weekend, so I knew the tattoos were words, but I'd forgotten about them and seeing his body again right now, I suddenly feel… a little lost, I guess.

I touch the first letter, then trace the whole sentence with my finger, reading it out loud. "'If you can dream—and not make dreams your master; If you can think—and not make thoughts your aim; If you can meet with Triumph and Disaster—And treat those two impostors just the same.'" I look up at him and meet his eyes. "That's beautiful."

"It's about you," he says.

"No, it isn't." I laugh. "It's Rudyard Kipling talking to his son about being true to oneself."

"I know that," Aiden says. "But when I got it, I chose the words for you. Because I dreamed one day you could be mine but I didn't want to lose everything with that gain. So if you're wondering why it took me so long, that's why. I wanted to win, but not at the expense of others."

"You wanted me to come to you," I say.

"No. That's not it at all. I just wanted it to happen naturally. If it was meant to be, it was meant to be. Because if it did happen naturally, then I knew that we'd all still be friends in the end."

"And if it didn't?" I ask.

He frowns a little. "I tried to be grateful for what I had. To be grateful that you were my friend. And if that's all you were ever gonna be, I'd feel a little cheated. But I just accepted that things would work out and tried to live my life. And look," he says, pulling my blouse down my arms so it flutters to the floor. He palms my breasts again, squeezing them harder this time. "Here we are."

"Here we are," I echo, pushing his shirt over his wide, muscled shoulders. There's more script tattoos. More writing. Probably more poems. And I want to read each one of them. Get lost in the words written across his body.

But later.

Now I just want him.

He closes his eyes for an extended moment. Like he's enjoying the feeling of my fingertips tracing words across his chest. I watch him. I watch every expression, every twitch and see every desire, every craving before he opens them a second later.

He's still holding the vibrator in his hand. It's still humming, and even though that noise seemed to fade into the background since we left the bathroom, it's back now. Reminding us what will happen next.

We reach for each other's pants at the same. My fingers fumbling with his button, his fingers deftly popping mine.

We pull down zippers, and reach inside. I feel two things in that moment. His fingers slipping past the waistband of my panties and sliding between my legs. And his hard, thick cock in my palm.

"Yes?" he asks.

"Absolutely yes," I reply.

He turns me so the back of my knees are pressed up against the bed, then lowers himself down into a crouch, pulling down my pants and underwear at the same time.

He leans in, grabbing hold of my thighs as he presses his mouth right between my legs. His tongue darts out, sweeping up between my pussy lips until he finds my clit. He flicks his tongue, hitting my sweet spot each time, and my fingers automatically thread through his hair. Fisting it and holding him there.

"Sit down," he says, pausing just long enough to get the words out before returning to his mission.

I do and he spreads my legs open and pushes my knees up to gain better access. And the next few moments are nothing but pure bliss. His forearms press again my inner thighs as his fingers part my lips. And then his open mouth covers my pussy. Sucking, and twirling his tongue, and tilting his head just the right way.

"Oh, shit," I mumble, arching my back a little. "Shit."

Because it feels so good and I never want it to end.

But just when I think it can't possibly get any better a finger slips inside me, turning upward as he finds the secret spot inside that triggers the most delicious feelings ever.

"Aiden," I moan. Unsure if I'm begging him to keep going or to put me out of my erotic misery and just fuck me now.

"Shhh," he murmurs, mouth still where it belongs, so that the vibrations from his hushing reverberate into my body.

He pushes another finger inside me—or maybe it's two more—because the stretching feels painful and lovely at the same time.

"You can come any time you want, Kali. I won't fuck you until you do that at least once from my mouth. But don't worry, I can make you come again. So let go. Just let go and just enjoy yourself. Because I'm dying to be inside you right now."

I want to tell him to just do that. Just fuck me now. But he's right. He can make me come again.

So I drift off. Just immerse myself in the experience. Let my body take over my mind and stop thinking about life, or the real world, or the future.

Who cares?

He nips my clit and I suck in a breath of air in surprise. It didn't hurt, not exactly. I'm too turned on to feel pain in the moment. Instead it makes me tingle and hiss out air through my teeth.

And then the vibrator is there—and, "Oh, God. Oh, Jesus Christ. Holy shit," I hear myself saying. He pulls it away and I whine. "No."

But then his tongue is back in place and his fingers are pumping me now. Not hard, but harder. Sliding in and out easily because I'm so wet. I'm so—

"Ohhhh," I say, bucking my back and writhing on the mattress. "Ohhhhhh." I see shooting stars and blurred lines as the climax peaks and the release is epic and penetrating. He pumps me harder as my pussy contracts, and relaxes, then contracts again.

The cascading waves of pleasure move through my body from my hips up. Tingling my skin and peaking my nipples until they are so hard and erect, I place my hands over them and squeeze.

"Jesus," I finally manage, turning my head to the side to pant in relief, even though the residual contractions are still happening.

But before I'm even finished Aiden is pressing the vibrator up to my clit. The sensation is almost overwhelming. Almost too much. My hand sweeps down to push it away, but he grabs me by the wrist and holds it against my belly.

"Do it again, Kali," Aiden says in a deep, throaty voice filled with desire. "Do it again."

This time the feelings are so intense I clench my teeth and wince. "Oh, my God," I say. "Oh, shit. That feels so…"

But I can't finish. I don't have any words in my head. I don't even know my own name. This lust, this hunger, this yearning for more overtakes me and I come again. This time I spasm, my whole body jerking as the universe vanishes and becomes nothing but light and dark in the same moment.

I lose time then. I don't know if I pass out from the pleasure or I nod off in exhaustion, but the next thing I know Aiden is crawling up the bed, my body between his legs. His cock dragging alongside my inner thigh until he's directly over the top of me. Hair hanging down in his face as I look up. Arms straight and palms pressed into the mattress. Chest hovering above my breasts as he leans down to kiss me with a hungry, open mouth and presses the tip of his cock right into my slippery entrance.

His fingers felt good. His mouth was amazing. But his cock is my God in that moment. I'm unsure where I'm at when he pushes deep inside me. I'm unsure who I am. I know nothing but the feeling of his long, hard shaft sliding up into my pussy until his tip touches my soul and he stops.

"Don't stop," I say.

He chuckles and says, "That's as far as it'll go."

"No," I whisper, shaking my head back and forth. "Try harder."

He thrusts. Just once. But it's quick, and forceful.

"Ah," I squeak from the pain. But I feel his power. I feel his strength and his love and I want more. "More," I say. "Do it again and don't stop."

He eases back, then thrusts again. And again I squeak out my pleasure. "More," I beg. "More."

He does it again, then again, then again until he's pounding me so hard I'm being pushed up the bed. His hips move quickly. Each time his punishing thrusts make me gasp. I grip his shoulders with tight fists, digging my fingernails into his flesh.

He grimaces and… slows.

"No," I say. "Keep going."

But he leans down and kisses me, whispering, "We've got our whole lives, Kali."

Do we? I wonder.

"We do, I promise," he says, reading my mind. And then he begins to move again. This time slower. Thoughtful and careful as he enters and pulls back. I begin moving with him and he sighs. "Yes. Like that. That's how I want it."

I wrap my legs around his hips and slide my hands over his back as he lowers himself down onto his forearms.

"I love you," he says, arching his back and sinking his face into my neck so he can whisper it against my ear. "I have always loved you."

I press my cheek into his and say it back. "I love you too."

And then there is a moment when all the stars align and the world turns upside down. When black is white, and off is on, and nothing and everything makes sense in the same instant.

And in that instant we come together.

CHAPTER FIFTEEN

I don't remember the last time I fell asleep so early in the evening, but then again, what did I expect when my whole week has been nothing but weird hours? All I remember now, the next morning, is that I rolled off Kali, pulled her into a tight embrace, and everything else but us faded to black.

But now it's seven AM, Kali is snoring softly in the bedroom and I'm standing in front of her living room window looking out on her city.

It's nice from seven stories up. Mostly quiet. A few traffic noises leak up, but not a lot since it's Saturday. I try to envision myself moving here with her. I could do that. I could probably just make Clyde the manager of Custom Crawlers and show up once or twice a week to check on shit.

But… this place is not my place.

It reminds me of my childhood before Bob became my dad. When it was just my mom and I, and we were nothing but products of this city.

It wasn't really a bad time. But compared to the life back in my adopted home town it was shit.

That's the only word I have for it.

How can you compare the woods, and the rocks, and the tadpoles to this?

I look up and down the street, taking in the neighborhood. Coffee shops, restaurants, little grocery stores. But I have all that back in my town too. And it's all close because I live above the garage in downtown.

Then I try to picture Kali living there with me and can't quite see that either.

I'm holding the envelope my dad gave me yesterday at the reading of the will. My name written across the front in Kyle's handwriting. I'm afraid to open it even though I know there's nothing inside but a phone number to call.

I want to make that call and then again, I don't. I have no clue what hearing Kyle's voice would do to me. Will it send me into a new depression? Because that's what that was last week. Pure manic depression. I tore apart his Jeep, for fuck's sake. Like the Jeep is a living thing and I'm holding it accountable for its actions.

And it's not even mine, it's Kali's now.

Guilt.

That's what this is about. Guilt.

Last night felt so good. So perfect. So inevitable.

But the next day always looks different.

All the doubts are back. All the misgivings and uncertainties come rushing forward with the rising sun, exposing them once again.

I look at the envelope, then turn it over and break the seal on the back, pulling out the single sheet of paper.

Just a number, that's it. Ten digits and nothing more.

My phone is in my back pocket so I pull it out, press the numbers, and hold it up to my ear.

There's a few clicking sounds, then a man's voice saying, "Welcome to Dead Notes, where your loved ones have an eternal voice. You're being connected now."

There's more clicks and beeps, then Kyle's voice.

"Dude." He laughs. "Dude! What the fuck happened? I hope to God I went out fucking a girl, or in a fight, or at fucking rock concert. Or on the trail, ya know, crushed by the Jeep because—"

I end the call.

Oh, fuck that. No fucking way. Fuck that.

I can't do it. I just can't. My best friend died last week and now he's on my phone.

I don't know what kind of sick asshole makes an app like this, but if he was here in front of me, I'd take a swing at him.

This is some sick, sick shit, that's what this is. Sick shit.

I run my finger through my hair, catching my own reflection in the window.

"Who the fuck are you?" I ask the stranger staring back. "What kind of asshole fucks his best friend's sister after his funeral?"

He doesn't answer. But he doesn't have to.

I'm that asshole.

I turn away from the stranger and flop down on Kali's couch. Leaning over, head in hands, wondering what I should do.

Keep her? I want to keep her so bad.

Or keep Kyle?

I feel like I have to make a choice. It's always been this way, so how could it ever be any different?

Kyle always knew I had a crush on Kali. Right back to the very first day we met. I remember that day so clearly. Like it was yesterday. My mom and I moved into the townhouse alone at first. She was dating my stepdad at that time, but still working for him. And he encouraged her to move closer to work, insisting it would be a better place for me to grow up.

And he was right. I came from this city but I do not belong here anymore.

Kali was the first kid I saw when I opened the door onto the townhouse green space and looked around. She was sitting in the grass picking buttercups. Tying them into some kind of chain. Wearing one of those perfect little-girl summer dresses I love so much.

But she looked up and smiled. "Who are you?" she said.

I stepped out onto the porch, the sunbaked concrete burning my feet a little, then hopped my way over to the cool grass and stopped, shading my eyes from the sun so I could see her better. Dark hair up in two braids that fell over her shoulders. Wide eyes and round face with pink cheeks. I felt like I had tunnel vision for a second. Like she was the only thing existing in the entire world. "Who are you?" I asked back.

I was a tough little shit back then. Fresh from an inner-city neighborhood where no one was really friendly and if they were, it was because they wanted to see if you had money and if you could be pushed around and bullied into handing it over. I wasn't bullied, but I did my share of bullying. Fighting, too. So I was rude right out of the gate.

But she didn't even pick up on it. I think I realized in that moment that this place was different. That these people out here lived by another set of rules. But if I didn't realize it before she said, "I'm Kali and you should be my friend," I did immediately after. Because that's when Kyle came up to us and stuck out his hands.

"Hi, neighbor," he said. "I'm Kyle and this is my sister."

"Hi," I said. "I'm Aiden." But I wasn't looking at him, I was looking at her.

And Kyle said, "You can be her friend too but you're my friend first."

I glanced over at him, and even though I was too young to really understand what that meant, I knew what that meant.

You're my friend first was just eight-year-old talk for, *She's off limits.*

Five minutes later we were in the woods, walking down a smooth dirt path that led to a makeshift, half-dead fort.

You're my friend first.

The very first rule we ever lived by and so… what the fuck am I doing here?

I don't know. But I have such an urge to go outside I quietly go back into Kali's room, find my shirt and shoes, and get dressed.

When I stand up from putting on my shoes I see myself in the window again. But for a moment I see Kyle instead. His face staring back at me instead of mine. His voice on the phone saying, "Dude, what the fuck happened?"

And I don't know how to answer him. I don't know what to say. So I just say the truth. That's all I got. "I love her."

Kyle says nothing. I want to believe that's because he's not here, he's dead. But I can't quite manage it. Because if he were here I know exactly what he'd say.

You're my friend first. She's off limits.

A few minutes later I'm walking out the door.

CHAPTER SIXTEEN

I dream about us. Not just Aiden and me, but all three of us. And we are all young still, for some reason. Late teens, maybe. Right around the time I started to notice Aiden was getting muscles and hair on his face. Right about the time I started to notice he was noticing me in the same way.

That day I stepped out of the shower, I realize. That's what I'm dreaming about. How it could've gone different if I hadn't called down to Kyle. It was a mean thing to do since I was the one making a move on Aiden and not the other way around.

But I can't help wondering what would've happened to us if I had just let him look. Or even invited him into my room.

Would we have kissed? I was naked, so would he have touched me? Would we have gone all the way?

Surely not. And even in my dream I can't get us that far around the bases. I didn't date anyone until I moved away for chef's school and even then, it was another year before I lost my virginity.

I was saving myself for you, Aiden.

That's what I say in my dream.

But of course, that was just the teenage romantic in me. He wasn't mine. He was never mine. Aiden always belonged to Kyle.

This thought wakes me up and I slip into that in-between world where you're still in your dream thoughts but also hearing the real world around you.

Traffic down on the street. Someone shouting. A horn honks. A beeping truck backing up.

I roll over and realize I'm in bed alone.

"Shit," I say, sitting up. "Aiden?" I call. No answer. I swing my legs out of bed, grab my robe off a chair, and slip it on as I wander down the hallway to the living room.

"Aiden?" I call again.

But my apartment isn't that big. Just one bedroom and the front room, which acts as a living room, dining room, and kitchen all mashed up into the same space.

I glance at the bathroom door, hopeful.

But it's open.

"Aiden?" I call again, realizing this is stupid. Because he's gone.

Jesus Christ. "What the fuck?"

But then that inner voice—that rational one that only shows up when I'm making a big deal out of something I shouldn't—says, *Payback, Kali.*

And it's right. Because I did this to him one week ago exactly. I slipped out in the early morning and never said a word.

It's just… I thought… we had…

But I was wrong. We didn't come to any kind of agreement. We had sex, just like last time. Granted, this time we weren't drunk, but—"Fuck!"

The door swings open and Aiden walks in. "Oh, good. You're awake," he says, tossing my keys into the little dish by the door.

"Where the hell did you go?"

He holds up a paper bag and a coffee holder with two coffees in it.

"Oh," I say, relief flooding through my body.

He cocks his head at me and smiles. "You thought I bailed, didn't you?"

"No," I lie.

He sets the bag and coffee down on the table and walks towards me. Maybe struts is a better word, because he's grinning and reaching for me as he approaches. He pulls me into an embrace, his hands caressing the smooth satin of my pale yellow robe, untying the waist as he laughs.

"What's so funny?" I ask, pushing his hands away. I'm not mad, not really. I have nothing to be mad about. He went and got us breakfast and coffee. But I'm irritated because, yes, I thought he bailed. I thought he was teaching me—

"Kali," he says, leaning in to kiss my neck.

"What?"

"I'm not going anywhere."

I sigh and lean into him a little. "I know," I say. "It's just… I had a moment, ya know."

"Oh, I know," he says, pulling back and brushing my hair away from my face. "I had that same moment last weekend."

"Sorry," I say. "I'm really sorry. I just… there was a lot of crap inside my head last weekend and—"

"You don't have to apologize. We needed this week to just calm down and find a new normal, right?"

I let out a long exhale. "Right. So do you think we're there?"

"Do you?"

I shake my head.

"Me either. But it's OK. We've got time to sort it out."

"I don't want to play games, ya know? I don't want to tease you, or you tease me."

"I've never teased you," he says.

"I know. But I was dreaming about that day you saw me getting out of the shower and—"

"Oh." He laughs. "Yeah." He runs his fingers through his hair, grinning. "You got me that day."

"I'm sorry about that too," I say.

"Oh, don't be. I already told you. That was the highlight of my life up until last weekend. And this weekend trumps the last one by miles. You hungry?" he asks. "You have to be hungry. We didn't even eat dinner last night. Just passed out."

"Yeah," I say, looking him over. He's dressed in yesterday's clothes, so his shirt is a little wrinkled, and it's not tucked in so the smart-casual office style has been replaced with morning-after-fuck style, but I like it. He shaved again for the reading of the will but this morning there's a shadow across his jaw that makes him ten times sexier than ever.

"I know what you're thinking."

"What am I thinking?" I ask.

He cocks his head at me. "My answer is yes. We can take a shower and have a little fun. But the coffee's getting cold, so…" He walks over, grabs the coffee and bag of food, and then sits on the couch. "Sit with me and let's eat, and talk, and forget about everything but the minute we're in right now."

I walk over, unable to hide my smile, and sit on the other side of the couch and put my feet up.

"I'm naked under this robe, Aiden Edwards." I spread my legs a little and give him a flash. "So are you sure you wouldn't rather do these things in the opposite order?"

He grins and takes out my breakfast sandwich. "You are very tempting, Kali Anderson. And while I do enjoy a peek with my coffee, you need to keep your strength up if we're going to win the gold medal in shower-sex gymnastics in thirty minutes."

"Promises, promises," I muse, taking a bite of my food. "Mmmm," I say. "This is good."

We eat in silence for a few minutes. Just staring out the window. I can see our reflection in the glass and we look so normal. Both of us lounging on the couch having breakfast and coffee. Like other couples do. Or people who actually are couples do. This is definitely not one-night-stand territory. I mean, it could still be if he lived in the city and not two hours away with no ride home. I dunno, it feels normal. Good normal.

"So… I called my number right before I left," Aiden says, breaking the silence as he wipes his hands with a napkin and tosses his breakfast wrapper onto the coffee table.

It takes me a second to figure out what he's talking about. But then it all comes rushing back. "Oh," I say. "How'd it go?"

"I hung up on him," Aiden says. Then laughs. Then frowns. Then looks at me. "It was hard, to be honest. Hearing his voice and knowing he's gone… I dunno. It's just…hard. Are you gonna to listen to yours?"

I nod my head and toss my wrapper onto the table next to his. "Eventually. Not now though. I don't think I could get through it without crying. The last week has worn me out, ya know? And I have to leave for work in a little bit. So…"

"Totally understand." He sighs. "What time do you get off?"

"Four," I say.

"Is it far from here?"

"Only a few blocks."

"So I can pick you up from work and walk you home." He smiles at me, reaching for my feet, then rubbing them. "Then we can go out to dinner. A date, you know. Not just sex."

"A date," I say. "Our first date," I repeat, trying that out.

"But first," he says, crawling over my body and easing down to kiss my neck.

God, how does he always know just where to kiss me to make me tingle? "Hey," I say, placing a hand on his chest. "You promised me shower-sex gymnastics."

He nips my earlobe and I wiggle beneath him. "I did." Then he gets up and takes my hand, pulling me to my feet. He slips his hands inside my robe, pulling the belt all the way loose, and squeezes my breasts. "Undress me, Kali."

And that's all I need to hear.

The next thirty seconds is nothing but my fingers popping buttons on his shirt and his jeans. Nothing but him kicking off shoes and sliding pants down. Nothing but us, both naked, kissing our way into the bathroom and stepping into the shower. Nothing but his hands gripping my ass as he lifts me up and backs me into the tiled wall.

Then it's everything I ever wanted.

CHAPTER SEVENTEEN

I ease my cock inside her, fully aware that she has to go to work. Also fully aware that I don't care if she's late. I'm gonna take my time with Kali Anderson. Treat every moment with her as something special. Treat every touch like something we need—like air, or water, or food. And treat every kiss as a gift.

"No games," I say, pressing her back up against the shower wall.

"Deal," she moans, her legs wrapping around me. Both of my hands gripping her ass, then one slides down to caress her leg.

I fuck her so slow it's agony and ecstasy in the same moment. This position lets me really feel her. Every strain on her muscles, every breath she takes in and lets out.

We move slowly at first, our bodies slippery from the water pouring out of the rain shower above us. It runs down my back, mostly shielding her. But her cheeks have little droplets on them, her lips so delicious and wet I kiss them. But soon that's not enough for her. She grips my upper arms tight, leaning back so I can push myself deeper and deeper inside her with every thrust forward.

This gives me space to flatten my hand on her stomach and slide my thumb down to her clit.

I rub it. Little circles that flick her nub back and forth. And she moans, suddenly straightening up. "Take me over to the bench," she says. "I want to ride you."

I swing her around, making her clutch on tightly, and do as she commands. She smiles, taking my face in both her hands, and positions herself so she can be the one to fuck me this time.

She's so fucking pretty. Such a pretty, pretty thing. I want to say that, but she's moving on me now. Slowly moving her hips back and forth across my lap as I grip her ass, then raise my hand and give her a smack.

It's loud in the shower and she squeals. "I like that," she says. "Do it again."

Oh, Lord. Help me. She is perfect.

I smack her again and she begins bouncing in my lap, her tits jiggling and bobbing to our new, faster rhythm. I grab one hard, unable to stop myself, and lift it up to my mouth. I swirl my tongue around her nipple, flicking it and nipping it as she lifts up higher and slams herself back down into my lap. I'm still holding her one breast, but the other one joins the ride, bouncing solo in a way that turns me on so bad, I suddenly have the urge to come inside her right this instant.

"Do it," she says. "Come for me, Aiden."

"When you ask like that—" I start to say, but I don't get much farther. She owns me right now. Totally owns me and her wish is my command.

She knows it too. Because her pussy tightens around my shaft and in that same instant I explode. Moaning, and hugging her tightly, and closing my eyes, wondering how I ever got so lucky to have Kali Anderson all to myself.

She lets out a long breath and rests her head on my shoulder as my fingertips tease out a pattern on her wet, slippery back.

"Perfect," she says, nuzzling her face into my neck.

"So perfect," I say.

I wash her hair after that. She's in a hurry now, realizing she has to be to work in forty-five minutes. But I take my time anyway, thoroughly massaging the shampoo in, then washing her breasts and stomach with soap as she stands under the rain shower to rinse her hair.

I take the same care with the conditioner. And she washes me with soap, taking extra care with my cock. I get hard again but when I shoot her a look, she shakes her head and says, "You're gonna have to wait until after our date tonight."

Shit, I think to myself. *I'll be jerking off the second you step out the door.*

And then everything goes too fast. We're done, drying off, getting dressed. She's wearing her chef's clothes. Black double-breasted coat with black slacks. And then a quick kiss and she's out the door.

I just stand in the middle of her living room and wonder how, in one week, my life could go from that to this?

But I know why and it breaks my heart to admit it.

Kyle died, that's how.

The rest of the day goes by slow. I walk around her neighborhood, looking for a good place to take her tonight, and settle on a French place just a few blocks south of her building. Then I stop at the park and take out my phone. I stare at the number I put in for Kyle earlier and wonder if I should just rip the Band-Aid off and listen to it.

"Man," I say out loud. "I wish you were here, I really do." I feel kinda stupid for talking to myself in the park, but it's the city. People expect this kind of shit. So I go on. "I really wish you could just… give us your blessing so we could respect you and still love each other at the same time."

Of course, there's no answer. Just thoughts in my head. Most of them negative. Kyle being pissed. Kyle never speaking to me again. Kyle refusing to be my friend.

If he was alive, and Kali and I were together, it would probably go one of those three ways.

But… there's always a chance it could go another way. Kyle could be happy for us. Kyle could wish us well. Kyle could say, "Now we're really and truly brothers," after I married his sister and made it official.

"Why is this so hard?" I ask myself. I don't even believe in God, or ghosts, or spirit realms or anything like that. So why do I care? He's gone.

But I look down at my watch and realize it's almost four and I have to go meet Kali.

I arrive just a few minutes early and tell one of the girls at the front I'm waiting for Kali when she tries to ask how many in my party.

Kali appears a few minutes later, smiling when she sees me waiting. "You really came to pick me up?" She laughs.

"I said I would."

"I know but… I just figured you were just being nice."

"I get to hold your hand all the way home, are you kidding me? I've been wanting to walk you home from somewhere for decades."

She leans up and kisses me, then blushes and smiles at her hostess friend and we walk out holding hands.

"What's for dinner? Please tell me not pasta or steak."

"French," I say. "And not the weird kind of French, either."

"Is there any other kind?" she jokes.

"You'll see."

"You know what the best part about working in a kitchen is?" she asks.

"What's that?"

"It's pretty much the law that you have to take a shower when you get home."

"Is it?" I laugh.

"Yes." She waggles her eyebrows at me. "Wanna join me?"

"Have you been thinking about our shower sex all day?"

"Haven't you?" she quips.

"I have," I lie. Because if I don't say that she'll wonder what I did think about and that's off the table tonight. No Kyle. Nothing that has anything to do with him for one night. "But I'm gonna decline the shower sex and hold out for the after-first-date sex."

"Oh." She laughs. "Well, I might be a little disappointed but I suppose I'll live if I have to wait."

I stretch out on her couch as she showers and gets ready. Breaking my own rule the second she disappears behind her bathroom door because I start thinking about Kyle.

I stare at my phone. Call that number sixteen times, at least, hanging up every time it gets to the part where he says, "… crushed by the Jeep because…"

Because I can't do it. I just can't do it.

My phone rings as I'm staring at it. But then I realize it's not my phone, it's Kali's, sitting on the coffee table where she put it down when we got here.

"Is that my phone?" she calls from the bedroom.

"Yeah," I say, looking down at her screen. "It's your parents."

"Answer it for me, will you?"

"Sure," I say, picking up her phone and tabbing accept, then putting it on speaker. "Kali's phone, this is Aiden."

"Aiden," her father says. "I'm so glad you two are together. Kali's nearby, right?"

"What's he need?" Kali calls.

"Yeah, she's here. Why?"

"We have something we want to share with you two," Kali's mother says. I must be on speaker phone too. "Kali, can you hear me?"

Kali comes out of her bedroom calling, "Yeah, I can hear you, Mom. What's up?"

"We want you to hear Kyle's message to us. We thought you'd love it as much as we did."

Kali and I look at each other with the same amount of dread. This is not how we wanted to start our date. In fact, we're both playing head-in-the-sand about this whole Kyle thing.

But of course we both say, "Yes," and "Great," because her parents need this moment from us and there's no way to back out now.

CHAPTER EIGHTEEN

"Where are you two?" my dad asks.

"Are you at the garage?" my mom follows up.

Aiden and I look at each other and shrug. "No," I say. "Aiden's with me at my place."

"Oh, that's good," my mom says. "I'm glad you two are together. Did you listen to your messages yet?"

"No," Aiden and I say at the same time. And then we're silent. Everyone is silent. And that makes the whole thing awkward.

"Oh, OK," my mom says. "Are you ready?"

I can say with one hundred percent certainty that we are not ready. But again, we both say, "Yes."

"Here we go," my dad says.

And then Kyle's voice is coming through the phone.

"Heeeeeey," he says. "Mom and Dad. I know this is a sad occasion for you but for me, you know, it's just another day. I saw this app online a couple months ago. Dead Notes. Kinda morbid. But you know, also, kinda nice. I don't know what happened to me. I do hope I died doing something cool, for sure. But I'm sorry I'm gone and you've got to deal with all that. Except I'm not gone, you guys. I'm right down the street at work. Aiden is downstairs. I can hear him and Clyde messing around and laughing. And I called up Kali the other day just to hear her voice because she's so busy living her life now, ya know. I have to record Aiden's message next and I know exactly what to say to him, but Kali. I had to think on that for a few days. Needed to hear her voice."

I try to think back to when he might've recorded this. When I talked to him on some random occasion that turns out wasn't really random.

I remember now. It was almost two years ago, just after I got hired at my current job. Kyle called me just as I was leaving for work and we talked as I walked. About what? I don't remember. Normal stuff. I was thinking about normal stuff and he was thinking about dying. He showed up at my apartment a few days later for no reason at all. No reason. Just wanted to take his sister out to lunch.

This was why.

"So I left you my house," Kyle continues. "I know you don't need a house, but someone will and you'll know what to do with it. Anyway, this is supposed to be profound and all that and so far it's pretty boring. But it's weird talking to you in the future. I'm going to assume everyone is sad." He stops to laugh. "Because I'm such an awesome dude. But what I really want to tell you is that… I love you." He chokes up a little and takes a breath. "I really, really love you guys. All of you. Kali and Aiden too. Even Clyde and the guys downstairs. However it was that I died, I need you two to know that you did a good job. That I was happy. Yes, like everyone I had bad days, but I was happy. And I know you're right down the street and I can end this recording and go see you myself—and I will, believe me. I've never wanted to hug you both so much as I do right now—but for some reason I feel like you're gone and not me. Stupid, I know. And selfish. I always was kinda selfish. Anyway, I know you're sad but don't be, OK?" he continues. "Please know that you're the best family a kid could ever ask for. Kali is the best sister, Aiden is the best friend… and life, you know? It doesn't get any better than that."

Kyle stops to take a breath, then lets it out slowly. "So goodbye. I guess that's all I have left to say, just… goodbye. Oh." He brightens a little. "And I sprang for the pro package of Dead Notes, which means you can leave me a message back. As many as you want, for as long as you want. I got you covered."

I swear to God, I can hear him smiling.

"So do that. For sure. Because my Dead Notes account is paid in full for twenty years. If you need longer than that… well"—he chuckles—"get a life, OK?"

I'm wiping tears off my face, but this is so Kyle I'm smiling with him.

"That's it," he says. "I just love you. And… thank you. Your son, in this life and whatever comes next. Kyle."

There's a few moments of silence. Well, sniffling, so not silence. And then my dad says, "Your mother is crying again," even though it's clear he's crying too.

"He was a good boy," my mom says.

"The best," Aiden whispers.

"Anywho," my dad says, trying to force a cheerful mood. "I know it's hard to hear him knowing that he's gone forever now. But you two should listen to your messages."

"Your dad and I weren't sure we'd ever get over this, Kali," my mom says, still sniffling. "We couldn't imagine a life going forward without your brother. But this helped, sweetie. It really did. So don't wait too long. He had something to say to you. And you too, Aiden. Let him have his last words."

"We will," Aiden says. Because there's a prolonged moment of silence after my mom finishes talking where I'm supposed to answer her, but I don't. "Maybe tonight," Aiden assures her, looking at me.

"Good," my dad says. "Well, I don't know what you two have planned but have a good time."

"And sorry if we ruined it," my mom adds.

I get my act together and say, "You didn't ruin it, Mom. You made everything perfect. Thanks for letting us listen in. I'll let you listen to my message after I'm done."

"You can listen to mine too," Aiden says. "For sure."

"Thanks," my mom says, still sniffling like crazy. "Now go do something fun. Go do something Kyle would do."

I nod and say, "We will, Mom. See you soon, I promise."

After Aiden ends the call we just stare at each other, unable to process what just happened. But I don't want this moment to fade, so I say, "My brother was an asshole genius."

Aiden laughs, wiping his eyes. "He totally was. Both those things."

"Who buys an app called Dead Notes?"

"Him," Aiden says.

"Him," I agree.

"Change of plans," Aiden says.

"What do you mean? We're not going out?"

"Oh, we're going out. We're going out Kyle-and-Kali-and-Aiden-style though."

"Oh, God. You're gonna make me build a fort, aren't you?"

We both laugh. Then he pulls me in for a kiss and says, "Trust me. I know what Kyle likes."

"I do trust you," I say. "There is no other person alive I trust more than you, Aiden Edwards."

"Good," he says, smacking my ass. "Now go get dressed. And wear jeans and sneakers. This isn't gonna be a fancy night."

I turn and walk down the hallway to my room thinking about him, and me, and Kyle. And all the fun kid stuff we used to do. All the innocent trouble we got into over the years. Hitting balls through windows, crashing bikes into parked cars, climbing trees and stealing forbidden fruit.

No, it won't be anything fancy. We're not fancy people.

That makes me look around my bedroom and sigh. My perfectly neutral color scheme. My modern, yet classic furniture. What happened to me? Where did I lose myself? Where did my past go?

I don't know, but I'm ready to find it again.

CHAPTER NINETEEN

Dinner was the wrong move. Fancy French restaurants aren't our thing. At least it wasn't. Maybe Kali has changed. It's possible she's even changed so much this won't interest her anymore. But if she's the girl I fell in love with all those years ago, then this is what a good time looks like.

Tonight I'm wearing the only outfit I have. Faded jeans, favorite boots, plain white t-shirt. Kali keeps staring at my arms in the car, enamored—I think—with the sight of my tattoos. I'm driving, since this is a surprise, so I can't look at her the way I'd like.

But I don't need to look at her to see her. I could close my eyes and see Kali Anderson's face no matter where I was or what I was doing.

Tonight she looks more like the girl I knew and less like the girl I don't. Her jeans are designer and her top is a flirty pink tank with off-the-shoulder ruffles for straps.

"When did you start getting those?" Kali says.

"What?"

"The tattoos."

"Oh," I say, looking down at my arms. "I dunno. Twenty-two, maybe?"

"Twenty-two," she echoes. "Wow. I've really been avoiding you, haven't I?"

I look at her and wink. "It's all good. We're here now."

"I didn't even know," she says, not quite feeling my all-good attitude. "It's like you turned into this other guy while I was away and—" But then she stops. "No. No, that's not it. It's like I turned in to this other girl while I was away and you… you just naturally became who you really are."

"Funny you should say that," I tell her. "Because the tattoos, all the writing, you know? It was a way to remind me of who I was. There was a time when Kyle and I weren't seeing eye to eye on the business. I wanted to make it bigger. Expand. Maybe into the city. But Kyle never did. He said we're good enough. People will come to us. I didn't believe him back then, but he was right. People come from all over to hire us, or buy Jeeps from us. Hell, we sold one to Japan a couple years ago."

"You had bigger dreams?" Kali asks.

"I guess," I say. "Or maybe I just wanted an excuse to see you." I glance over at her and wink.

"You could've come to see me any time, you know."

"And you could've come home."

"Hmmm," she says. "So what made you change your mind? About expanding?"

"You got a boyfriend," I say.

"What year was this?"

"Two years after Kyle graduated."

"Oh," she says. "That guy. Didn't last long. Only about eight months. I've never been in a long-term relationship. Have you?"

"Not really. I dated a girl from a crawler competition once. On and off for a couple years. But her family's shop was based in Utah so it was mostly casual hook-ups when we had time."

"You didn't love her?"

"Nah," I say, glancing at her again. "You're the only one I could see myself with, Kal. It's always been you."

"Why didn't you say something? I mean, God. I would've loved to know that. I would've made an effort."

"See," I say, "that's the thing. It shouldn't have to be an effort. I knew as long as you were in the city doing your thing, living your dream"—she laughs, but I continue—"it was never gonna work. And I figured… I'd rather wait for the perfect time than risk us ruining the idea. If that makes sense. In my mind you and me, we were always a possibility, ya know? And if we gave it a try and failed, then that was it. It always felt like there was just one chance. I don't know why, that's just how it felt. It took us a while, but I think this is our chance."

I flick my turn signal and Kali looks out the window to where we're going. We're well outside the city limits, but not even halfway back to our home town.

"Go-karts?" She laughs. "Oh, man. This place brings back memories."

Which was the whole point. I know that wasn't the plan. The plan was no Kyle this weekend. But it was a dumb plan. He's part of us. He will *always* be part of us.

As soon as Kyle and I got his Jeep running during our teens this is where we'd go on the summer weekends. Kyle was always looking for girls with our other high-school friends. Always looking for romance. But Kali and I would just buy a night's worth of rides and race around the track. Hours and hours of racing, and laughing, and friendly competition. I figured Kyle was

OK with that. We weren't really alone together. Couldn't even talk. It was all about meaningful glances across the track as we did our best to beat each other across the finish line. And then, when we ran out of rides, it was about playing pinball and videos games.

It was always too hot in there, and always too crowded, and always too loud. But it was fun. And we knew what to expect from each other. It was familiar, I guess. The ride out here was always Kyle driving, Kali in the passenger seat, and me in the back. Leaning forward between their seats, arms resting on their headrests. And it made me feel like I was putting my arms around them. Like we were a team.

I pull into the parking lot and automatically find a space close to where Kyle always parked.

"I can't even believe this is still here," Kali exclaims. She's smiling and excited and I'm glad our plans changed from grown-up romance to teenage fun. "I didn't even think kids did stuff like this anymore. These days it's all smartphones and social media."

"They don't know what they're missing," I say. "Come on. I'm ready to kick your ass on the track."

We hold hands as we walk inside the arcade and stand in line at the ticket counter for the karts. There are quite a few kids but surprisingly, there are a lot of adults like us too. Maybe they used to come here as teenagers and are on first dates? Maybe we're not so different than other people? Maybe it takes growing up and growing apart to realize that the one you loved first is the only one you'll ever love for real?

I get us both a wrist band for unlimited kart rides and then we just… do our thing. Morph back into the old version of us, but better.

It's both surprising and sobering that I barely fit in this car now. It hits home just how much I've changed. But I feel the same now as I did back then.

Excited to be here with Kali. Thrilled as we laugh our way around the track. And proud of her every time she beats me.

We don't race anyone else. Never did. It was always just us out here.

When we get tired of that we order a pizza in the little snack bar area, then play some video games and skee ball. I was always better at that than Kali because I've played baseball since I was six, but she was always better at pinball.

In the end I win her a bright blue teddy bear and she wins so many free games on pinball, we monopolize that machine for hours.

And then the place is closing. It's two in the morning and we're walking back to the car tired but smiling.

"That was the best date ever," Kali remarks as I pull out of the parking lot and head back to the city. "Thank you."

"You're welcome," I say.

"I felt like Kyle was here with us, you know? Like this is the kind of date he'd approve of."

I look over at her. She's got her head resting up against the window with her eyes closed. Light moves across her face as we pass under street lamps and for a moment we're back in time. Kids again. Driving home after the perfect Saturday night.

"I feel him too," I say. More to myself than her.

I miss him, I don't add.

I miss you, I tell him in my head. *I miss you so much. And I know I'm your friend first and I know she's always been off limits. But she's happy with me, Kyle. And I also know you'd want that.*

Wouldn't you?

Kali nods off after that and this makes me feel good for some reason. Like I'm taking care of her. Like it's my responsibility to get her home safe. Like I've taken over Kyle's job in his absence.

You can trust me, I tell him, continuing my mental conversation with my best friend. *I swear, Kyle. You can. I would never hurt her.*

He believes me, right? He knows me, doesn't he?

So why did he always feel this strongly about keeping us apart? Why didn't he ever change his mind?

Then I realize… maybe he did? Maybe somewhere in that phone message he left for me there's an addendum to the rules? Maybe he even gave me permission?

Kali wakes up just as I'm pulling into her parking garage. She wipes her long hair away from her face and says, "What'd I miss?"

I smile at her and turn the car off. "Come on," I say, "let's go to bed."

Because I'm feeling better about all this now. I feel like this night was a win, that we're both the people we were meant to be and maybe that's why getting together took so long, and… that Kyle really does approve of us.

And there is something in his last message to me that will prove me right.

CHAPTER TWENTY

Aiden takes me upstairs to my apartment. I feel exhausted and exhilarated at the same time. This was the perfect first date. So many good memories came rushing back to me while we were at the go-karts. And even though Kyle wasn't there, it felt like he was. It felt like no time has passed at all. Like we're all still teenagers with our whole lives ahead of us.

"Bed," I say, walking down the hallway like a zombie.

"Bed," Aiden agrees, following behind me, still holding my hand.

I don't even bother turning on the lights, just wait for Aiden to follow me in and turn to face him. There's light leaking in from the city outside. Just enough for me to see his chiseled face and shadow of stubble on his jaw. And of course, his blue-green eyes catch that light and glint with mischief.

"This was the best night I've had since… well, a very long time."

Aiden places his hands on my hips and bumps his forehead to mine. "Agreed. I feel good about it now, Kali."

He doesn't say it specifically, but he doesn't need to. He feels like he's gotten Kyle's approval. "I do too," I tell him back. "I really do."

I place my hands on his face, leaning up on my tiptoes to kiss him on the mouth. He kisses me back. Softly at first. A sweet kiss. Tender and loving. One that says this isn't about kissing, or sex, or teenage lust. It's about love, and friendship, and being meant for each other.

But of course, there's desire in there too. So much desire inside me for this man. He's my one. He's always been my one. And just because we grew apart for a while doesn't mean any of the feelings I've had for him over the years changed.

And if they did change, they only grew stronger. It's sad that it took the death of my brother to realize this, but there's still time.

I break away from our kiss and look up into his eyes. "There's still time," I tell him.

And because he knows me—and has always known me—he understands. "Plenty of time, pretty thing."

His hands slide up my arms, sending chills through my body, and then tug down on my off-the-shoulder top until I slide my arms out and it's bunched up at my waist.

"Nice shirt." He chuckles.

"I wore it just for you," I say. Kidding and serious in the same breath.

His hands go to my breasts, squeezing them through the cups of my strapless bra, and then he tugs that down to my waist too and my upper half is bare.

I reach for the hem of his t-shirt and he helps me lift it over his head. In the darkness I can see the writing all over his body.

"One day I'm gonna read all this," I say, tracing some letters with my fingertip. "I'm gonna read it so many times I'll have it all memorized."

"Or maybe I'll read it to you," he says, unbuttoning my jeans and pulling down the zipper. "One day, Kali Anderson, I'm gonna make you my wife. And on that night we take those vows I will tell you all the little things you've missed that are written on my body. But you won't be sad for missing them. You'll be happy for me, like I am for you, that we grew up, then apart, and came back together again."

My heart thumps in my chest at his words. His proposal that isn't quite a proposal, but still feels like one. At the range of emotion that's coursed through my body since we found each other again. At the laughter, and the tears, and the heartache that will one day become something sweet.

He bends down and starts taking off my sneakers. He places them neatly off to the side and reaches for the waist of my jeans, easing them carefully over my hips and dragging them down my legs until I step out. He folds them and places them on top of the shoes. Then without standing up, he unhooks my bra and slides it down my legs with my shirt. Again, artfully folding them up and placing them on top of my jeans. Like this care he's taking with my clothes is a metaphor for how he'll take care of me in the future.

And none of it seems trite, or planned, or fake.

He's just not that kind of man.

When that's done he leans forward, kissing his way up my belly as he stands up again. He doesn't tell me to undress him. Just begins taking off the rest of his clothes. He folds them and places then on top of mine.

And we stand there in the hazy city light leaking in from outside, and really look at each other. Maybe for the first time ever.

Bare, naked, and unashamed.

"God, I love you," he says, reaching for me. His hands find my hips and his mouth finds my lips, and then we're kissing again.

Open mouth. Twisting tongues. But still a slow, careful kind of kiss. A passionate kiss that says, *No. This is not typical, or ordinary, or without meaning.*

It says... *This is special. We are special.*

He takes half a step forward, eliminating any distance between us. Until our bodies touch. My breasts to his chest. His hips to mine. He's hard, but that's not even one of the first five things on my mind right now.

His face is on my mind. And his hands are on my mind. And his lips, and his tongue, and his heart are all on my mind in this moment.

"I've missed too many nights with you, Kali," he says. "I don't want to miss any more."

There's a conversation that comes after words like that. A conversation about logistics, and living arrangements. About jobs versus careers versus callings. About hometowns and city life and other things too. Like wedding days, and honeymoons, and maybe even children.

But not tonight. None of those things are important tonight.

So I say, "I don't want to miss any more either." And I say it because it's true. One hundred percent true. I don't know how we fit all the odd pieces of our separate lives into one coherent puzzle, I just know that if it's meant to be, it will be.

We will make it. Or maybe we won't have to make it? Maybe now that we know who we are to each other all those things that have been keeping us apart will give up the fight and surrender to fate.

Because I feel like that's what this is.

Fate.

Soulmates.

Aiden pulls back first, his eyes already open when I open mine. He smiles at me and says, "Let's go to bed." And then he leads me over to the bed, pulls back the covers and invites me to climb under them.

I do. Slowly and carefully as he follows my lead. Under the soft comforter he repositions his body so he's on his side. One fingertip dragging up and down my belly. Starting just above my pussy and ending right between my breasts.

My skin prickles up from the soft touch of his fingers, my nipples becoming hard and erect. He flicks one, then takes it between his fingertips and massages it gently.

I close my eyes and sigh, wondering how I could exist two hours away from him all these years. Two stupid hours apart. This could've been mine for years already.

"Kali," he says.

"Hmm?" I say.

"Tell me what you want. Tell me what you like. And don't be embarrassed or afraid because I need to know everything about you right now. I want to hear all of it."

"Oh, God," I say, smiling and unconsciously covering my face.

"No," he says, pulling my hand away and placing it between my legs. "I'm serious. Show me again how you like it."

I draw in a deep breath, then slip one finger between my pussy lips. Parting them slightly, acutely aware that I'm already wet. And then open my legs and grant myself full access.

Aiden leans over, kissing my belly, then rests his cheek on it. The slight stubble rubbing against my skin.

"Like this," I say, rubbing small circles around my clit with two fingers. "But faster. I'm just not very good at getting myself off without a vibrator."

"Do you want me to get that for you? Or should I take a whirl at it?"

I chuckle, my free hand automatically going to his head, tugging on his hair and hugging him at the same time. "Please, give it a whirl."

He picks up my hand between my legs and places it on his head to join the other one. "You can guide me, when the time is right."

He means… when he eats me out. He must like that feeling. Of being guided.

"But for now, just relax and let me do my thing."

"OK," I whisper. I have nothing else to say to him but yes tonight.

He starts by playing with me the same way I was playing with myself, rubbing small circles, but then one finger slips between my lips and he changes to a back-and-forth motion. Each time delving deeper between my legs until his fingers stop on my asshole.

"Ohhh," I say.

"Like that?" Aiden asks, bringing his fingers forward again.

"Mmm-hmmm," I moan. "Everything is so slow and soft. It's almost… agonizing."

"It's anticipation," he says. "More commonly known as foreplay."

I laugh, can't help myself. And then open my eyes and find him turning his head to look at me. "Well, you're very good at it."

"You deserve to know how I feel when we're being intimate," he says. "And this is just one way to show you."

"Considerate and careful, that's you."

"Not with everyone," he says. "But with you, always, Kali. I love your body, I think you're pretty, and yeah, I want to put my cock inside you and fuck your brains out. Pretty much have wanted that since we were sixteen. But that's not the point. It's just one way I can show you how I feel. And this," he says, easing his face forward until his tongue is flicking against my clit, "is another."

His words tickle and I hold my breath for a moment. Then he gets on his knees, repositions himself so he's between my legs, and drops his mouth down onto my clit. Sucking slowly and with just enough pressure to drive me wild.

I fist his hair, guiding him the way he wants me to. Moving his head as I bend my knees and open my legs to give him better access.

"Yes," I moan. "This definitely is another way to show me."

He doesn't reply. Too busy pleasuring me with his tongue and his lips. Too busy making sure I get everything I need from him tonight.

So I just enjoy it. Just let him take me to the height of pleasure. And when he says, "Come now, Kali. Come for me and let me taste you," I do.

I come.

It's a long, slow, pulsating orgasm. With my hips rising up to meet his mouth, and his tongue probing me, licking up my release.

And I vow, in this moment, to make sure he has the same experience.

CHAPTER TWENTY-ONE

She tastes sweet. Her release is slow, and long, and glorious. She moans as her body stiffens, her back arching off the bed as her fingers grip my hair and push my head down, trying to get more pressure, more friction, before it begins to subside.

When she's done she turns her head to the side, eyes closed and maybe a little bit tired. I make a decision and live with it. Because none of this was for me. It was all for her.

"We can go to sleep now if you're tired."

Her eyes fly open and she scowls at me. "No. Are you kidding? No."

I laugh.

"I'm serious. That would be a monumental breach of the love-making contract. I mean, maybe one day. There'll be a time when I take you up on that offer, but tonight? Oh, hell the fuck no, Aiden. I can't even believe—"

"Sorry," I say, still laughing.

"I mean, I need to do my part. That whole time you were eating me out I was thinking up ways to make you feel the way I do right now. Not because I feel obligated, but because I want to. I want you to know how much I love you. I need to show you."

"Hey," I say, crawling up her body, dragging my fully erect, throbbing cock over her leg. "I'm not gonna say no to that."

"Good," she says, placing both her hands on my cheeks and smiling. I love it when she does that. It makes me feel like she's looking at me, and only me. Like I've got her undivided attention and she wants mine too. "Then you lie down. Because I want to know how you like it now."

I waggle my eyebrows at her, even though it's mostly dark in here and she probably can't even see me, then roll off to the side and place my hands behind my head. "I'm ready."

"I hope so," she says, getting up on her knees and positioning herself between my legs, almost the way I did for her, except she stays on her knees.

God, I want to take a mental picture of this moment. "The only way this gets hotter," I say, kinda thinking out loud, "is if you turn on the lights."

She reaches over, flicks on the nightstand light, and says, "Your wish is granted."

Fuck. This girl just does it for me. Everything about her is special.

She leans back, her long, dark hair dragging across my chest, and looks me in the eyes as she takes my cock in her hand, gently tugging on it, and says, "Show me how you like it."

God. Damn.

I reach for my cock, wrapping my hand around hers, and pull upwards until the tip of my head disappears into her fist.

"Fuck," I say, closing my eyes. And I don't know why this is so hot. It's nothing unique or unusual. I could be jerking myself off like this any day of the week. Or she could be doing it herself and it would still feel good—but this. Us. Doing it together. Now I know how it must've felt for her when she was showing me how she likes to play with herself.

"Like this?" she asks. Looking pretty, and mischievous, and fiercely sexy in the same moment when I open my eyes.

"Harder," I say, squeezing her hand so she'll tighten her grip on my shaft. She does, pumping up and down. "Then tug it a little," I say, jerking on my cock.

She gets a rhythm going with my help and once she's got it I take my hand away and caress her forearm with my fingers.

"Feel good?" she asks.

"So good."

And before I even get the words out, she's lowering her mouth to the tip of my cock, covering it with her warm lips as her tongue darts out and sweeps around my head in a circle.

I grab her hair up, gathering it in both hands, making a pony tail, and hold it in one fist as I lift my head to see her better.

So much hotter than porn.

She smiles around my cock and then sucks a deep breath through her nose and goes down. Far down. More than half of my shaft disappears inside her mouth. Her lips sealing tightly around my dick as her tongue flattens out and presses against it as she comes back up and immediately goes back down.

That's it for me. I swear. Seeing Kali Anderson take my cock deep in her throat with the lights on is just about the highlight of my life right now.

Even though I want to keep watching I can't stop myself from resting my head back into the pillow and just enjoying how she makes me feel.

Not just the blow job. All of it. The date, the go-karts, the pizza, the games. I've missed this so much and now… she's mine.

She's really mine.

"You're mine," I whisper, as she continues to bob on my cock.

"All yours," she says, releasing her mouth from my cock just long enough to utter the words.

I urge her back down with my grip on her hair and she complies. Continuing to show me how much she cares with her mouth.

"Mmmmm," she hums, making the skin of my cock vibrate against her vocal cords.

I want to hold it in, not come yet because this feels too good, but I can't. So I start to bring her head up, letting her know I'm ready, but she just shakes her head, telling me no.

She wants me to come in her mouth again. Like she did that first night. Only this time she's not drunk.

Just thinking about this has me ready to explode. But then Kali takes me one step closer. Her hand slips down to my balls and begins to fondle them. Cupping them in her palm like a prize.

And that's it. I give up. I give in. She wins.

Because I release all my love and desire for her in long spurts that shoot across her tongue and down her throat.

I groan, tightening my grip on her hair as I hold her face close to my stomach.

And then I ease up and she releases me, breaking the seal of her lips, and begins kissing her way up my stomach.

She flops down to my slide, nuzzling her face into my neck. My arms wrap around her automatically, and I sigh. Content.

No. More than content.

Complete.

I dream about her. And me. And Kyle too. In my dream he's laughing and smiling. And I'm holding Kali's hand, so I get the feeling he approves. And then I drift away, realizing it's morning and I'm waking up.

My morning wood is typical, but then again, it's not. Because Kali is jerking me off.

"Oh, my God," I mutter. A little bit sleepy still, but mostly turned on. "You're gonna spoil me, Kal."

"Just trying to wake you up gently." She laughs, leaning in to kiss my cheek. "We fell asleep before we finished last night so I figured—what better way to make it up to you than this?"

"Oh, I can think of better ways." I grin, opening one eye, then closing it quickly because the summer sun is shining brightly into the windows.

"Hmmm," she coos. "Maybe this?" And then she swings her leg over mine and mounts me. Her hands deftly placing my cock up against her entrance.

"I could get used to his," I chuckle, grabbing her hips.

"A woman who knows you so well, she anticipates your morning needs?"

"No," I say, gazing up at her. "The one woman who loves me back and cares enough to surprise me every once in a while."

"Oh." She giggles. "Well, that's me, Aiden." And then she leans down to kiss my lips, just as she begins to rock back and forth.

There's no way this is going to be long, sensual, mind-blowing sex. It's too early, I'm too hard, and she's way too sexy and eager.

But still, it's the best ten minutes of my life. Waking up with Kali every morning would be a dream come true.

She comes first, and it takes every ounce of strength to make sure that happens, and then she lets me flip her over and fuck her hard for a little bit before I explode inside her.

When we're done I want to go back to sleep forever. I wrap her up in my arms and hold her tight, unwilling—or maybe unable—to let her go.

"I have to work today," she says.

"What time?"

"Noon."

"What time is it now?" I ask, unable to open my eyes.

"Ten-thirty."

"Shit," I say.

"You can just go back to sleep and I'll go to work and be home by eight. Then I can take you home."

I peek at her under one heavy eyelid.

"Or not," she says, laughing. "You can stay as long as you want, Aiden. I just figured you'd need to go back to work tomorrow."

"I probably should," I say. "But… I am the fucking boss." One hundred percent as of Friday, I don't add. "So I think I'll stay another day."

"Good," she says, climbing out of bed.

I open both eyes to look at her as she walks across the room, naked, and then disappears into the hallway.

"You know what we should do though?" she calls from the bathroom after she turns on the shower.

"What?"

"Listen to Kyle's messages." She pops her head back in through the bedroom door. "Don't you think?"

I nod my head, thinking back on my dream last night. "Yeah," I say, feeling better about that whole thing. "Yeah, we should."

She smiles at me, then disappears again. A few moments later she's in the shower and I'm forcing myself to sit up in bed. I lean over, grab my jeans and my phone falls out of my pocket.

I set it aside, pulling on my pants, and then grab it again and walk out to the kitchen to make us some coffee.

Just as I'm adding milk and sugar to our cups, Kali appears in her robe, towel-drying her hair. She takes the cup I hand her, sips, smiles with her eyes closed, and then opens them and says, "I'm ready. Play yours first."

CHAPTER TWENTY-TWO

I've watched Aiden struggle with Kyle's judgment all my life. I knew—maybe not as well as Aiden—but I got the message Kyle was sending loud and clear even though he never said it directly to me.

And it was just this one case where Kyle's opinion ruled. Just me, that's it. Any other time Aiden was free to do whatever he wanted. Even if he and Kyle disagreed, Kyle stood by him. If Aiden needed something, Kyle was there. And if Kyle needed Aiden, he didn't even have to ask for help.

They both bestowed the same loyalty on me. I realize now that I didn't just have one brother growing up, I had two.

"Are you ready?" I ask Aiden. Because he's been staring at the phone number on his screen for a few moments too long.

He nods his head, smiles weakly at me, then nods again. He presses the call button and it rings, but then, just as quick, Aiden ends the call.

"What are you doing? I thought you wanted to listen."

"I do," he says, running his fingers through his hair. "I don't know. Hearing him last night—" He looks at me. "That was fucking hard, ya know?"

"I know," I say. "The idea of leaving a message seems kinda cool when you first hear about it. In theory, you think, 'Yeah, that would be great to get one final message from my loved one after they die.' But in practice…" I shake my head. "I think… I think the first time through it's scary and hard. And I have a feeling my parents were bawling their eyes out the first time they listened. But then, after that initial sadness and shock fades a little, you realize it truly is a gift. We have this one last chance for him to say something just for us."

Aiden nods, then presses the button again. This time he gets as far as Kyle's first greeting before he ends the call again.

"We can do it later," I say. "After I get home from work."

Aiden just stares at his phone. Then shakes his head. "No, let's do it now. Together, too." He smiles at me. "I promise I won't be a pussy and hang up this time."

"Third time's a charm," I say, trying to smile.

"Third?" He laughs. "Shit, I think I've dialed this number about three dozen times already. But yeah. Definitely now. With you."

"Together," I say. Then I wrap my hands around his arm and lean into his shoulder as he presses the call button one last time and this time, he hands the phone to me when it rings.

"Don't give it back until he's done," Aiden says. "No matter what."

"I got you," I say, making a promise as I take the phone from him.

Then Kyle's voice fills the room. "Dude." He laughs. "Dude! What the fuck happened? I hope to God I went out fucking a girl, or in a fight, or at fucking rock concert. Or on the trail, ya know, crushed by the Jeep because that's the only way to go."

"Oh shit," I say, ending the call.

"See," Aiden says. Then he grabs his phone back and says, "Jesus Christ. We're both a bunch of pussies," as he presses the call button one more time. "This time we're putting it over here and neither of us is allowed to touch it. Clear?"

I nod, unable to stop my smile, and say, "Clear."

"OK," Aiden says, sighing with frustration as he walks back over to me and takes a seat on the couch.

"Dude," Kyle says. "Dude! What the fuck happened? I hope to God I went out fucking a girl, or in a fight, or at fucking rock concert. Or on the trail, ya know, crushed by the Jeep because that's the only way to go. Either way, you know. Sorry for the trouble. I know Kali is probably a mess and my parents are probably beside themselves. I know I am no older than thirty-seven because they say you gotta update the message every five years or when something changes your family situation, ya know. So you know who you're talking to and all… you know. So… fuck. I went young, I guess. I don't know what happened but I'm sorry I'm not there anymore."

My heart is swollen with sadness. Almost overfilling with grief. My brother… my twin… my literally other half is gone. It hits me harder to hear him talk about his own death than it did looking at his lifeless face at the funeral.

And it's so him. So very him to worry about *us*, when he's the one who's gone.

"I wanna…" Kyle continues. "I don't know. I want to talk forever right now. Tell you all sorts of shit. All the fun we had. Hey, you remember that fucking go-kart place out in the boondocks? God, I've been thinking of that place for like a week for some reason. Ever since I bought the Dead Notes app and started preparing my last call. We had so much fun there, didn't we? Kali loved it too. When I go—" But he stops. Then starts again. "Not when, I guess. Because I'm gone. But do me a favor, OK? Take Kali there one more time. Ride the karts, and play the games, and maybe, I dunno, win her a stuffed animal or something. Something blue, OK? Remember how she used to love blue? Not dark blue, that was for boys."

Kyle stops to laugh and I start to cry.

"Light blue. Her whole room was light blue. Anyway." Kyle sighs again. "Sucks, man. Thinking about death. I was gonna tell you about this the other day. For real, I was. Because I thought, ya know, if Aiden bailed on me I'd want a last message from him. I'd want to hear his voice again, just one more time. But I wouldn't want to know about it ahead of time. I don't know why, I just wouldn't. And I don't know how everyone feels about me doing this. Probably sad. Maybe it's morbid. I don't know. I just know that... if you go first, bro, I'd want this chance to hear you again. So I'm giving that to you. Oh, and hey, you know what? You can leave me a message back. Yeah, that's the best part. You can leave me messages for like twenty years. I bought the platinum package. So any time you ever have something you need to get off your chest, you call me, bro. I'm here, I swear. I'm watching from... wherever the fuck it is we go after this whole shit show called life ends. I'll listen," he says. Then his voices hitches a little, like he's crying too. "I'll always be here for you, understand? Brothers for life... and death too, turns out."

I glance at Aiden and find him bent over, elbows on knees, head in his hands.

"OK, then. I wanted to say more but… shit. I don't know what else to say. Just, I love you, man. You're the best friend ever. And I'm sorry. I'm sorry I checked out early. I really am." Kyle sighs. A long, sad, empty sigh. Then he says, "Later, bro."

I nod my head, unsure what to do now. Just feeling grateful, maybe? That he did this for us. And sad too, but it's so real now. That loss.

I walk over to the phone sitting on the table and I'm just about to pick it up when Kyle comes back. "Oh, hey, I forgot. One more thing. You were my friend first, remember that?" I can almost hear him smiling through death. Then he says it again, just to make his point. "You were my friend first."

Then there's a beep and Kyle's voice one more time. "Hey, you've got Kyle. I'm here, I promise. So leave me a message and I'll get back to you as soon as I can."

Another beep.

And then… silence. Because I end the call without saying a word.

I turn to look at Aiden. He's staring up at me with red, watery eyes. I say, "I'm gonna call in sick today."

But he shakes his head. "No. You're going to work, Kali. I'm fine, I promise."

And looking back on it now, I should've stayed. I should've told him no, I am not going to work. We're going to talk this through and get past it, and everything will be great.

But of course, I did go to work. Aiden walked me there himself.

And then two hours later he called me.

And he said, "I just can't do it, Kali. I just can't do this to him."

And even though he didn't explain, he didn't need to. I heard that last message from Kyle clear as day.

You were my friend first.

In other words…

Stay away from my sister.

CHAPTER TWENTY-THREE

I am a worthless piece of shit in more ways I can count. I knew. I knew all along that Kyle wanted me to stay away from Kali. He made one request of me. Just one.

Stay away from my sister.

That's all he ever demanded from me, ever since we were eight.

Just stay away from my sister.

All those times he was there for me, too. Any time I needed help, he was there. If I needed money, I didn't even have to ask. He just put some cash in an envelope and left it in my apartment. If I needed a hand with a car I was working on, there Kyle was, tools out, no questions or instructions necessary. If I got in a fight, he stood next to me, daring anyone to fuck with us.

Not me, *us.*

And the day we put him in the ground I jumped his sister. In her moment of weakness, and sadness, and need—I took advantage.

I was your friend first, Kyle. I was.

Until I wasn't.

After Kali left for work last Sunday I just kinda sat on her couch wondering how I let myself succumb to temptation. And the thought of him knowing, from the other side of some spectral place or wherever the fuck people's souls go when this shit is over, just the thought of him knowing this is how I disrespected our lifelong friendship—it kills me.

Because I didn't listen to his message and yet I took Kali to the one place he mentioned. We did everything he wanted us to do that night. We had fun. She smiled and laughed and so did I. I won her the stuffed animal. And then I brought her home and took her to bed.

God, what was I thinking?

I wasn't thinking. I was dreaming, that was my problem. Or I was in denial. Because I knew. I fucking knew it was wrong and I did it anyway. Talked myself into believing Kyle would approve when I knew damn well he wouldn't.

So I called Clyde and told him everything. Told him what I'd been doing, told him where I was, told him about Kyle's message and then I begged him to come pick me up from Kali's house.

I played the message for him as we drove home. Back to this small town, back to where I belong, away from the city, and Kali, and all the fanciful dreams I'd been having about a future with her.

I called Kali as I was waiting for Clyde to pick me up. That was a dick move too. At work. Just what the fuck, Aiden?

I could hear her confusion on the other end of the phone. Hear her pain and sadness.

I did this to her. I made her sad. Because I knew there was one fucking rule to follow and I decided not to.

She didn't call me back. I don't know what happened after that. Clyde pulled up to her building and I was waiting outside, so I just hopped in and away we went. Two hours later I was walking up to my apartment above the garage, thinking maybe I should just sell this place and move far, far away. Forget about love and happiness, and everything I let myself believe over the past week, and start over.

When Monday morning came I realized I'd been up all night thinking. Plotting my escape. But I was too tired to put any plans into motion so I just stayed up in my apartment until the compressors stopped humming down below and the garage went quiet again.

None of the guys bothered me that day. Probably hated my guts after Clyde told them I broke Kyle's golden rule.

But I went downstairs after that. Nothing else to do and I still had a Jeep to finish killing. I was still working on it when the guys showed up on Tuesday. This time Clyde took me aside and asked me if I was OK.

"OK?" I said, blankly looking at him. "No, I'm not OK."

He sighed, let me be. They all let me be. And I was still down there after they left for the day.

Exhaustion overtook me then and I went upstairs. Played Kyle's message over and over again. Downloaded it into my phone, then put it on repeat and listened for hours.

You were my friend first.

I didn't sleep that night. Not even a wink of sleep.

Thursday I almost called her. I told myself it was to apologize for soiling the memory of our friendship. But it wasn't.

I wanted to tell her I loved her. I wanted to make this ache in my heart go away. I wanted to be able to eat again. To sleep again. To think about something other than his stupid Jeep and the way I kissed her and made love to her and…

I feel like I lost her now too. That both my best friends are dead and I'm all alone.

I need to take a moment to pause here. To reflect on that and internalize it. Because it *sucks*. It fucking sucks so bad. How, in the course of just a few weeks, did I end up here? How did I lose so much, so fast?

And is there any way to save it?

And what is the "it" I'm trying to save?

I wish I knew, But I don't. I just know I feel empty and sad.

*That night—last night—*I slept for the first time in days. Crashed sitting up in a chair, Kyle's message still playing.

But when I woke up this morning it had stopped because my phone was out of battery.

I walk into the bathroom and flick on the light. Stare at myself in the mirror in horror. Because I look like a walking dead man. No shower all week, barely slept, didn't eat, stopped working, and talking, and living.

"Who the fuck are you?" I ask the stranger in the mirror.

And the answer I hear in my head is, *The guy who betrayed his best friend's last request. That's who.*

A knock at my apartment door makes me peek down the hall. "Who is it?" I yell.

"It's me," Clyde says, checking the door knob. Finding it unlocked, he opens it and walks in. "Just coming to make sure you're still alive. I called your phone and it went straight to voicemail." He stares at me for a moment. His expression unreadable. And says, "You look like shit."

I huff out a laugh. "Thanks, I didn't already know that."

"So…" Clyde says. "You coming to work today? Or what?"

"Nope," I say, walking into the kitchen to make a cup of coffee. Clyde waits as my little machine spits out dark brown liquid. I take a sip without bothering with sugar or milk.

"Well, that fucking Jeep has been on that lift for two weeks now and it's in the way. You've got a real fucking mess down there. When are you gonna deal with that thing?"

I shrug.

Clyde does one of those nods. The kind that's really just a chin lift, then a chin lower. The kind that says, *Uh-huh*, which he says out loud anyway. Then he sucks in a long breath and says, "Well, you know. You're being a dick about this."

"How do you figure?" I ask, taking another sip of coffee. "It's my garage. I can keep a car up on my lift in my own bay as long as I want."

He squints at me, pressing his lips together like he's trying not to wince. "Very true," he says. "But that's not what I'm talking about."

"Then make your point, Clyde. Because I'm busy here."

An eyebrow lift this time. "Busy, huh? OK. If you say so. I'm gonna state my piece and leave. And after that you do whatever the fuck you want."

"Go for it," I say.

"Kyle doesn't give a fuck about you and Kali, and you know how I know that?"

"How?" I ask, playing along as I continue to sip my coffee.

"Because he's dead. He's fucking gone, OK? I don't want to be harsh, but this bullshit needs to end. You need to take a fucking shower, change your smelly clothes, eat some goddamned breakfast, and get your ass downstairs where you belong. We've got ten jobs on the roster. There's a two-month wait to get anything done when people call. And you're up here worried about what a dead guy thinks of you dating his sister? Who, by the way, you've been in love with your entire life, even I can see that. Just… forget about Kyle. He's gone, Aiden. Gone. He's not haunting you with a stuffed animal. And for fuck's sake, erase that goddamned message."

"Fuck that," I say, feeling hot as my temper boils. "He was my—"

"I know," Clyde says. "But you're taking shit way too fucking literally. Can't you see?"

"See what?"

"He was fucking with you, Aiden. 'You were my friend first?' It was a joke, asshole. That's it. Just an inside joke to make you laugh."

"It wasn't a joke, Clyde. He said stay away from my sister."

"He did not say that! Are you fucking insane right now? Give me your phone, I'll prove it to you!"

"Battery's dead," I say.

"So put it on the charger. I'll prove it to you. You've gone crazy. You're making shit up right now. And fine, you wanna be sad about your best friend's death for a week or two? That's totally cool, man. I get it. I miss him too. It was hard for us too. But this is week three and you're not getting better, you're getting worse. That's not sad, that's depressed. And if you don't get your ass in that shower and do all that other shit I just told you to do, I'm calling your parents and letting them know you're not handling this well and they should keep an eye on you."

"Keep an eye on me?" I laugh.

Clyde shrugs. Then he whispers, "This is crazy, Aiden. You are officially living in Crazy Town." Then he exhales a long, frustrated sigh and says, "Delete that message and move on."

I stare at him for a few moments and watch him walk out.

Who the fuck does he think he is? Just who?

My best friend had one rule. A rule he very clearly spelled out in his last message.

Didn't he?

I go find a charger, plug in my phone, and listen to it again. Then again, trying not to read into things. Then again, this time being as detached as I can.

"Oh, hey, I forgot," Kyle's voice says. "One more thing. You were my friend first, remember that? You were my friend first."

Clyde's right. He didn't say, *Stay away from my sister.* I added that in because that's what comes next. That's what *always* came next.

I have so many questions. So many things to say to this asshole, ya know? Was that a joke? Was it a joke the whole time? Did I just spend twenty-six years reading between lines and looking for things that never existed? Making it all about me?

I play the message one more time, and this time I wait for the beep and start talking.

"Uh… hey, man," I say into the phone. "So… fuck. I miss you." I have to stop there for a few seconds because my throat is all tight and it's suddenly hard to swallow. But I have to get this off my chest. I have to. Clyde is right. I can't live like this. I don't know what comes next, I just know something *has* to come next. "I have to tell you something, OK? And you're not gonna like it. But I need you to know that…"

I stop again. I have every intention of telling him what Kali and I have been up to. Every intention of confessing all my transgressions.

But instead I say, "… I love your sister. I love Kali, Kyle. I've always loved her. And I'm sorry if that bugs you and if you want to hate me for that, it's all good. It's cool. Your prerogative. But I'm gonna hang up now. And I'm not gonna call you back, ever again. I'm just gonna let you go." I pull the phone away from my face and I'm just about to tap end when I sigh and realize I can't do it. I just can't walk away like this.

So I take a seat on the couch, put the phone back up to my face… and keep talking.

I talk forever. Going fast at first because I have a bad feeling about this message. Like any second it's gonna beep and say, "Messages are full." But it didn't. It just let me talk. I keep him on the line for hours.

All day, in fact. And when I finally run out of things to say it's dark outside. And my heart is heavy and sad.

But you know what?

My conscience is clear.

And then I go down to the garage and get back to work on Kyle's Jeep.

CHAPTER TWENTY-FOUR

Alison is holding my hand as she leads me down the street to her apartment. She showed up at my place this afternoon looking for me because she went by my work at lunch and they told her I quit.

Yes. I quit. I don't know what's wrong with me. I don't know how to fix it, I just know I can't work there anymore. I need to do something else. Maybe that means going back to school and learning something new, or just getting in my car and driving west until I hit the desert and my car breaks down so I have to get a waitressing job to make ends meet, or moving back in with my parents and pretending I'm a kid again.

I don't know. I don't care.

Life just… sucks.

"OK," Alison says. "We're here."

"You got a new apartment?" I ask, then revise, because this isn't an apartment. It's a whole townhouse. Like a big one. Four stories tall plus a garden level. "How did I not know about this?"

"I told you I was moving… *that* day. But you probably don't remember."

"Oh." I sigh. Then I feel guilty for missing out on her big news because Kyle died. Because this place is definitely better than the last one.

"Don't get too excited. It's not really mine."

"What do you mean?"

"I mean, it's my parents' house."

"What? You moved back home? Jesus, Alison. Why didn't you tell me?"

She shrugs. "Kyle, ya know. You've been having a rough time."

"Well, clearly I'm not the only one."

"It's not as dire as it sounds," Alison says. "I told you a few weeks ago I wanted to open a new business, remember?"

"Uh… yeah. I remember." I say this as I rack my brain for details I've obviously discarded. "Bakery, right?"

"Right! And I have the perfect plan!"

"We can't afford the retail space, Alison. It's too expensive."

"We won't need it."

"How do you figure? We need a real kitchen. A good one with two ovens and—"

"Welcome to my rich parents' home," Alison says, sweeping her hand at the fancy townhouse. "I only have two sisters at home now. Everyone else is either married or in college. So guess what?"

"What?"

"No guess!"

"Alison, I can't guess. It could be anything."

"OK, I'll tell you." And then she jumps up and down a little so her beautiful curly hair bobs around her perfect face. "We have a whole apartment in the garden level. My older sister was still living down there when I was a teenager, so I never got a chance to fully experience it, but now my baby sister lives on the fourth floor, and my older baby sister lives on the third floor, so the whole apartment is just sitting empty." She clasps her hands together and squees. "And my parents put in a brand-new kitchen for me so I could bake!"

"Seriously?"

"It's only temporary. They said six months and then I either have to pay the full rent or they're gonna kick me out. Because they really renovated it to have an income property. They're just excited I finally have some ambition. But listen, Kali, we could do this in six months, I swear, we could. Just come inside and listen to my plan."

I side-eye her as I consider what she's offering me. Which sounds a lot like a partnership.

So I do go inside with her. Because I need the distraction and her excitement is infectious. And the kitchen is beautiful. Fully renovated, stainless-steel everything, soapstone countertops perfect for rolling out dough, and a huge double oven that can probably bake six dozen cupcakes at the same time.

"So what do you think?" she says, once she finally stops talking.

"Mail-order baked goods," I say.

"Yes! Everyone's doing it. There's a shop online called America's Bakery and you just open up your online shop and put up pictures of what you're baking each month, and people order from you. And my third oldest sister, remember her? Ami?"

"You stole her boyfriend, right?"

"Yeah, her. Well, she's a social media genius. Does the accounts for everyone who's anyone in the city. And she said she'd help us do our socials and get us started."

I take a deep breath, then sigh. "I mean, it sounds great, but—"

"But what?"

"I tried this already. It didn't work."

"You didn't have me!" Alison exclaims.

"I did so!"

"As an assistant, not a partner. Now you've got me as your partner. You bake, I do the accounts and marketing. It's gonna work, Kali. I know it. Just say yes. You can move in here with me too! There's two bedrooms. Plenty of room."

"What happens in six months?" I ask.

"Look," she says, grabbing my arms with both hands. "No one knows what's gonna happen in six months. We could come up with seven different ways it might go and none of them will be what actually happens. So get over it. We're doing this. And in six months… who knows. Take a risk with me, Kali. I promise, whatever happens will be better than this. You don't even have a job anymore."

She's right. In fact, Alison is looking a lot like Prince Charming right now. Riding in on her parents' huge townhouse and saving me from certain misery.

So I say, "Fuck it. I'm in."

She jumps up and down and claps her hands and starts talking about being roommates, and how much fun we're gonna have, and—

"What's wrong?" she asks. "You're not excited?"

"I am," I say. "I totally am. And thank you so much for thinking of me."

"Shit, bitch. You're the baker. I'm just the marketing hack. But… seriously, what's going on with you?"

So we sit down at the counter of our new kitchen and I tell her everything that's happened since she sent that text to Aiden for me a couple weeks ago. And then I end it with 'the message' from Kyle and Aiden disappearing.

"Jesus," she says. "Why didn't you call me?"

"I dunno. I was too sad. And I didn't want to call just to mope and complain."

Alison smiles at me. A warm, best-friend kind of smile. And I realize in this moment, she *is* my best friend. What started as just a business relationship has truly morphed into something bigger. "Kali, that's what I'm for. That's what best friends do. One of them gets to complain while the other one listens. So this message from Kyle. What did yours say?"

"I don't know."

"What do you mean you don't know? You didn't even listen to it?"

"No." I shake my head. "I'm too afraid of what he's gonna say."

"Oh, Kali," Alison says, pulling me into a hug. "I'm so sorry you're going through all of this. And look at me, all excited and thinking about the future. I'm such a bad friend."

"Shit," I say, sniffling into her perfect hair. "You're the complete opposite of bad friend. You're the best."

She stands back, hands on my shoulders, holding me at arm's length. "You need to listen to that message. Like… now."

"I want to, I do. But… not now, OK? I need to do that alone. And I'm not ready to go home yet. I just want to sit here with you and dream a little first, OK?"

"Yes," she says, squeezing my shoulders. "Yes. That sounds like a perfect plan."

She shows me around the apartment. The whole place comes furnished and guess what? It's even my style. No modern couches, no stainless-steel tables, no blank, blah neutral color scheme either.

My room, the one Alison says is mine, is even decorated in light blue. Light blue with tan accents. It's girly, but in a grown-up way. Kinda like me. Or the me I used to be. And wouldn't it be fantastic to be the old me again? The carefree one who wore pretty dresses and still made forts with her brother and his best friend in the woods. The one who would have her hair up in perfect braids and could still climb rocks and catch frogs. The one Aiden and Kyle remember.

After hours of talking she calls me a car and walks me out to the curb, arm linked in mine. Because we are truly partners now. I'm going home to give notice to my landlord and put all my furniture up for sale online. Because I don't need that fake stuff anymore. The new, real me is about to be born.

All the way home I begin to dream. Begin to see things in a new way.

I had no clue Alison came from such a wealthy family. My family isn't poor by any means. We've never had money problems, but this… this is a real opportunity for us to start over. And isn't that what I really need?

It's not just the fact that I can't have Aiden. It's not just the fact that Kyle is dead. Or that I'm sad about both those things.

It's more than that.

I'm adrift. I have no direction, I have no goals, and I let my dream fade because of one failure.

Alison is one of those people who doesn't believe in failure. She believes in chances. Second chances, specifically.

And not only that, I let myself fade too.

I want *me* back.

When *I get home* I kick off my shoes and sit on the couch with my phone in hand.

I'm going to do it. I'm going to listen to Kyle's final message for me. And no matter what it says, I'm not going to think about it again.

This is it. The end of my sadness starts now.

I press the number into my phone and put it on speaker.

"Kali," Kyle's voice says. It's not the 'hey, dude' greeting that Aiden got, that's for sure. It's low, and a little bit sad. And before he even starts talking again, I'm crying.

"Kal," he says, his sadness so clear. I am his twin. I feel what he feels. He swallows hard. Hard enough for me to hear him. Then sighs and says, "I feel like crying right now. Not because I'm dead and you're alive, but because I miss you already and we're both still here. And I know how I'd feel if you were the one to die, so I know exactly how you feel right now, sis."

I nod my head. Because I know how he'd feel too.

"First," he says, drawing in a deep breath. "I love you. I love you so much. More than anything or anyone in this entire world. You are my other half, Kal. My other half. No one could ever replace you. I don't think I got married, but if I did, not even my wife could take your place in my heart. You are my number one, you hear me? My number one."

Tears are streaming down my face. Like rivers. Like waterfalls.

"And I want to say all the things. I want to talk to you forever. You're the reason I got this app, Kal. You. Because I want to have conversations with you forever. I want you to call this number, any time you want, and tell me anything at all. Tell me everything. I want to know all of it. Every bad day you have, every good day you have, every milestone, every new friend, every new guy. I want to hear about your wedding day, and your babies when they're born, and even when you're old, I want to hear about that too. Because I still need you, OK? And you still need me. So…"

He's crying now too. But he takes a moment to sniff and I know he's wiping his eyes. I've seen him cry enough over the years to picture all this in my head.

"So…" he continues. "One more thing before I let you go for now. And it's about Aiden."

"Oh, God," I say out loud. "Here it comes."

"I know what you're thinking. I know what I've said over the years. But listen to me, Aiden… he's… he's been in love with you since the first day he met us. I saw it, Kal. I saw the look on his face that day and I knew—that was it. This city kid was gonna grow up and marry my sister one day."

I shake my head. "No," I say. "That's not gonna happen."

But of course, this is a one-way conversation so I can't reassure him. I can't tell him that it's OK. Aiden and I would never do that to him.

"And I want you to know," Kyle continues, "that… I approve."

"What?" I say.

"I approve," Kyle says. Like he's here in the room with me. Right this very second. "I didn't make Aiden my best friend because I was afraid he'd take you away, Kal. I made him my best friend so I could watch you two fall in love. So I could witness it happening and know, one hundred percent in my heart, that you got the best guy on this whole planet. And if I ever did die before you, I'd rest easy knowing Aiden was the one left behind with you. Also… you know… I might've taken it a little too far a few times." He manages a sort of laugh. Then takes a deep breath. "And maybe, back when we were teenagers I kinda meant it too. Like that necklace he gave you. Remember that? Yeah, I freaked out. And it was a real freak out. But it was just teenage jealousy, Kal. I was being immature and stupid. I was afraid I'd lose you both. I knew it at the time too. And I should've apologized but it's hard to be mature when

225

you're fourteen, right?" He laughs again. "But," he says. His voice softening. "I'd like to apologize now, if that's OK. And tell you one more thing about Aiden Edwards."

"What?" I say again.

"Give him a chance, Kal. He's a good guy. And you two need each other right now. So just give him a chance. When opportunity knocks, just… open the door. All you gotta do is just open the door."

I'm stunned silent. He approves? He knew? He wants us to be together?

Kyle sucks in a deep breath, then says, "OK, that's it. I'm outta here. But don't forget, OK? Don't forget to tell me everything. I really, *really* am listening." There's another pause and he says, "Later, sis. I love you."

Then there's a beep so I can leave a message, but at the same time, there's a knock on my door.

And the only thing running through my mind is Kyle's last request.

Just… open the door.

Kali opens the door, tears streaming down her face. "What's wrong?" I ask, grabbing her shoulders. "What happened?"

She sniffs, then bows her head, then looks up at me and blurts, "I just listened to Kyle's message."

"Oh." I deflate a little. "Oh," I say again.

"He's…" She wipes her eyes. "He's the best brother ever and I miss him so much!" She wails that last part and I instinctively pull her into my arms.

"I'm sorry, Kali. I'm so, so sorry." I hold her face tightly to my chest, never wanting to let her go again.

She struggles and pushes back and I have a moment of panic. She's rejecting me. Kyle had his say and now she's gonna choose him over me.

I bow my head and sigh. "It's OK," I say. "I understand."

"No, Aiden," she says. "You don't understand at all." Then she wipes the tears off her face with both hands and says, "Come inside. Just… listen." And she grabs my hand and tugs me through the door.

"No," I say. "You listen, OK? You listen to me right now. I have something to say and I'm gonna say it. And then… then whatever you want to do, whatever you decide, I'll live with it. But just let me get this out."

She blinks at me three times quickly. "OK."

"OK," I say, straightening out my t-shirt. Then I swallow and take a deep breath, and on the exhale, I speak.

"I love Kyle. He's my brother. In life and in death. Nothing can ever change that. But I love you too, Kali. And he loves you. And me. And I know, deep in my heart, that no matter what Kyle thought about us being together, he would want us both to be happy. So I'm sorry if he doesn't approve. When I see him in the afterlife, or next life, or wherever the fuck it is people go after this place, I'll make my case to him. I tell him how much I love you. How I've always loved you since that very first day I saw you back when we were eight. And I'll tell him I respected his wishes, all these years. And I didn't plan on hooking up with you after the funeral, it was just… it was just fate, OK? It was.

"We're meant to be together. You, and me, and Kyle. But he's gone, and there's no way in hell—no way in fucking hell—he'd rather us be apart than together, no matter what his feelings were before he died.

"So listen to me," I say, grabbing her face with both hands and looking into her eyes. "Listen to me right now. Hear me, OK? I love you and from now on, I don't care what anyone thinks about that, I'm gonna keep loving you. And if you don't love me back, fine. I'll live with it. Because I'll have to. I won't like it, and I won't be happy about it, but I'll live with it. But if I had my way, Kali Anderson, I'd marry you today. Right the fuck now. I'd drag your ass down to the courthouse and make you my wife, and then I'd put you on a plane, and whisk you off somewhere special, and then we'd make babies. All right? That's it. That's what we'd do. Get married, fuck on a tropical beach, and make babies. So there! What do you think about all that?"

She's covering her mouth with her hand.

Appalled?

Surprised?

Shocked?

"What?" I say. "What are you thinking? What... are you *laughing* at me?"

She starts to giggle, then holds up one finger. "Wait right here. No," she says, closing her apartment door, taking my hand, and tugging me behind her. "Come with me."

She grabs her phone off the couch and holds it up.

I stare at the screen, not understanding. "Who's on the line?"

"Kyle," she says. "It's Kyle. And you just said all that to him."

"O-kaaay," I say. Then, "Well, good. Good. I'm glad he heard me. Because I meant every word. If he loved us, and he did, then he wants us to be happy. And being happy means—"

"Aiden," she whispers, leaning up to kiss me on the lips. "He does. He said so on my message. Let me play it for you."

She puts the phone up to her ear and says, "Kyle? Aiden's here now. I'm gonna hang up so he can hear your message too. But I'll call back. I have so much to talk to you about."

Kali looks at me, then the phone, and she calls Kyle again.

I take a seat on her couch and listen. Hear every word. I cry, I smile, I laugh. I think I rollercoaster through every emotion possible.

"He always knew, didn't he?"

"He did," Kali assures me. "And do you even realize that you knocked on my door just moments after he told me to open it?"

I sigh. It's a sigh of relief. I'm not looking for signals. I'm not looking for meaning, or destiny—and I don't believe in much. I'm not religious, I'm not even really spiritual. I don't believe in aliens, or ghosts, or vampires.

But I believe in Kyle.

I believe in Kali. And me.

I believe in *us*.

Kali sits next to me on the couch, then climbs into my lap, both arms around my neck so she can lean her forehead against mine.

And then she says, "Yes."

"To which part?" I ask.

"All of it, Aiden. Every single thing. Just yes."

I grin and decide to tease her. "OK, you just said yes to marriage, and kids, and moving back home."

"Moving back home…"

"I'm kidding," I say. "But not really."

"Hmmm…" she says, slowly tracing a finger down my chest. When she get to the hem of my shirt, she lifts it up and the moment her skin touches mine I get a chill. Not the bad kind. Not the kind that makes your gut clench because something's wrong.

But the good kind. The kind that makes your heart swell, and ache, and open up because it feels so right.

I reach for Kali's face, placing my hands on both sides of her head so I can guide her into my kiss. She responds exactly how she's supposed to. Eager, slow, tender kissing.

She rolls the front of my t-shirt up my chest and I lift my arms so she can take it off. She reaches for the hem of her tank top and pulls it up over her head too. Both of them are tossed aside without another thought.

She sits here, in my lap, hands on my shoulders, beautiful breasts in my face—and she says, "Let's start now."

I grin at her and say, "Which part?"

And she says, "All of it," as her hands dip down to pop the button on my jeans. "Lean your head back and close your eyes, Aiden. I'm gonna take care of you first."

I smile, but do exactly as she says. Because Kali is a gift and I'm going to accept her with grace.

She gets down on her knees between my legs and pulls my zipper down. Thirty seconds ago I was not thinking about sex but now… "Oh, God," I sigh, as her mouth dips down to kiss the bulge in my pants.

A moment later she's pulling off my boots, then dragging my pants down my legs. And then I'm sitting naked on Kali Anderson's couch as she pumps my cock with both hands.

I crack one eye open and she's smiling up at me. "You're peeking," she says.

"I can't help it," I say, threading my fingers into her hair. "I want to look at you."

"Nope," she says. "Nope. I just want you to relax and enjoy it. Then, when I'm done with you, you can look all you want."

I smile and close my eyes. And I swear, it feels like all the tension, and sadness, and anxiety over the past few weeks just melts away the moment she covers the tip of my cock with her mouth and seals her lips around me.

Slowly she takes me deeper. One hand reaching up to my chest. Flat on the tattooed words that runs along my side and under my arm. Her other hand on the top of my thigh as she sinks her mouth down over my shaft.

I have an urge to pull her hair and smack her ass but I calm that urge. Tell that urge to back off for now.

Reassure that urge that she said yes and there are a thousand and one nights of this in our future.

Now both of her hands are on my thighs, pressing down on them as she bobs her head up and down, letting her slick, wet tongue slide along my cock.

I don't want to come yet. I want to wait and hold it all in. I want to savor this moment and the way she feels. I want to open my eyes and take a mental snapshot of her between my legs. I want… I want… I just want her and I want her forever.

But in that moment she reaches up with one hand. Slides up my chest until she's gripping my shoulder. And she eases off me, just the tip of my dick in her mouth, and begins to suck. Pulsing up and down it— just the tip—as she draws everything out of me and I let go.

I just let go.

I let go of the past, of the future, of expectations and disappointments. I let go of everything and just live in the moment with this one, perfect woman. The one put here on this earth just for me.

"You can open your eyes now," Kali whispers.

I do. A part of me expecting this to be a dream. Expecting her to disappear. But no, she's there. Grinning at me. A little bit of come on her lips.

I reach over, swipe it up with the tip of my fingers, and she opens her mouth and licks it off.

Sometimes, these past few weeks, I wonder what I missed. What parts of her growing into this beautiful woman did I miss because I was so loyal to her brother I couldn't even wrap my head around the idea of us being together?

But you know what I've finally realized?

I didn't miss a thing. Not one thing. Kali, as she is right now, is perfect.

We are ready for our future.

Kali stands up, takes off her bra, wiggles out of her shorts, climbs back into my lap, and wraps her hands around my neck.

We are naked. Bare. Unashamed. And in love.

One hundred percent in love.

CHAPTER TWENTY-SIX

Even though our romantic relationship is new, it feels like we've been together forever. Going down on Aiden isn't about going down on him. It's not about taking him in my mouth and sucking him off until he comes. It's not about whether or not I'll swallow or if he's going to return the favor when I'm done.

It's not about any of that.

It's about the urge inside me to be near him. To be skin to skin. Matching our breaths and heartbeats.

It's about trust and friendship.

It's about being whole and complete.

It's about sharing. Each other, this life, this love. All of that. So I sit in his lap, fully aware that we are naked. Fully conscious that this is our beginning. Fully comfortable with what I just did and what comes next.

But also understanding that we have time. That we can go slow, if we want. That this isn't about sex at all. It's about connection.

I trace the writing on his body as I gaze down into his eyes. "Want me to read it for you?" he asks.

"You have it all memorized?" I ask.

"Of course," he says. "I put these words on my body for a reason."

I nod my head slowly. "Then yeah, read it to me."

He looks down at his chest. Then over to the right. There's a passage under his right arm and he repositions himself so I can see it. "'To war with yourself is to fight against instinct.'" He pauses for a moment, then says, "And I wrote that because…" He looks at me. "Because of you, I guess. All these years I knew there was something missing and now I know what it was. You."

He looks down again, pointing to another string of words. "And this one, here," he says, pointing to the words across his chest. "It says, 'You can climb to the top of the mountain and still not see the stars.'"

"I like that one," I say. Because I've read it before. During sex my eyes couldn't help but see the letters and unconsciously read the words.

"It means that sometimes what you're looking for isn't the prize you thought it was."

"Did you write all these?" I ask.

"Only some," he says. "At first I'd use other people's words but then I realized… it's my body. It's my art, I guess. So I wrote my own after that." He leans forward to kiss me, his hands reaching for my breasts. Gently squeezing them in his palms. "You are the stars for me, Kali. And getting you here in this moment was like climbing a mountain in some ways. But in other ways it was easy. Because really, all I had to do was show up."

"I love you," I say. The urge inside me to tell him this is overwhelming. "I've always been yours."

He hugs me tightly then. I place my head on his shoulder and hug him back. Resting, finally. Because for the first time in my life I feel whole and complete. Like there is no obstacle in my way. No hurdle to get over.

He caresses my back with his fingertips. Gently passing them up and down my spine until that chill he always seems to find shoots through my body.

I feel him starting to get hard again underneath me, his cock pressing against my inner thigh. "More?" he asks.

"So much more," I say, lifting my hips and taking him in my hand. I place him at my entrance and close my eyes when he enters me. Then I sit down in his lap, my back arched over his chest, my forehead resting against his, and we begin to move.

It doesn't take much. That's something I've learned about us. It doesn't need to be hard, or fast, or punishing in order to climb that mountain and see those stars.

Just slight movements are enough. Inches, that's all it takes. Just a few inches of forward shift fills me with excitement.

This is how we make love.

Slowly.

Carefully.

Tenderly.

And the climax isn't about bursting explosions or fireworks going off.

It's more like… happiness sinking into my soul.

"Kali," he says, as we come together.

"Yes," I say. "My answer is just… yes."

Later, after we shower and eat, I tell him all about Alison's plan. All about the new venture we have in mind and how I'm going to move out of this place and share an apartment with her so we can get the business off the ground.

He smiles at me the whole time. Holding me close in bed as our day winds down. Confident that no matter what, we will work out.

But after he falls asleep I have one more thing to do before I can rest. So I get up, put on my robe, and take my phone out into the living room.

I take a few minutes to collect my thoughts, then dial Kyle's new number.

Just saying those words in my head makes me feel better. Kyle's new number.

He's not gone.

I mean, I hadn't seen him in a long time before he died and he wasn't gone. So even though he's dead now, he's still here. And this phone number proves it.

I listen to his message again. Not with sadness this time. Not with apprehension. But just so I can hear his voice. Appreciate the way he sounds. How, when he recorded this, he was having a good day. I know this without knowing. He's my twin, my other half, and his voice is filled with everything I loved about my brother.

After that's over I wait for the beep and start talking.

"Kyle," I say, smiling into the phone. "God. OK. I can do this. I've decided you're not gone. And, no. I'm not delusional, I can just feel you still, so as long as I know you're in my heart, you're here. I don't know where that is, but it doesn't matter. So I hope you're OK with me calling you. I think my life is about to change and I'm gonna wanna tell you everything. Just like old times, right?"

I settle into the couch cushions, bringing my legs up as I lean my head back. Like I would settle for any long conversation.

And I tell him everything. All the things that have been happening. Not just since he died, but before that too. Catching him up on my life.

And even though he doesn't talk back—this is a true, one-sided conversation—it feels normal. Like no matter what, this message will find its way to him eventually.

It's like writing letters, I guess. You put your thoughts down on paper and then send it out into the world, never knowing when it will arrive at its intended destination. Never knowing if it will be read. Never knowing if it will be answered.

But none of that matters. You send that letter on faith. Because you have things to say and you can't keep them in.

That's what this is.

I'm writing Kyle letters with my voice and sending them out into the world—to some cloud server, I guess. Trusting that one day he'll get my message.

When I'm done it's nearly three in the morning. I'm not sure if I just hang up or what, so I press pound for some reason. And then Kyle's voice comes on again and he says, "Thanks, sis. Now, if you want to hear more from me, just press nine."

"What?" I say.

"I made hundreds of messages for you, Kali." Kyle says this like he heard me. "I have two years' worth of messages for you saved up. One day you'll have heard them all, but until then, pretty sister… just enjoy. Enjoy everything, Kal. All of it."

I swipe new tears away from my cheeks and then…

I press nine.

I have one more problem.

The Jeep.

It was on the lift for another couple weeks before I started seriously thinking about what to do with it. Every time I came downstairs to work Clyde would side-eye me, then the Jeep on the lift, then me again. Sending me not-so-subtle messages to get that thing out of here.

But he didn't say anything. It's like he knew I was trying to figure it all out and just let me think.

But in the end I decided not to kill it. It wasn't mine to kill in the first place, it's Kali's Jeep now. But I'd like to think I'm it's true parent since I did build the thing. And Kali didn't interfere when I said I had an idea. She patted my shoulder and said, "Surprise me."

At first I was just gonna put it back together and give it a paint job. But then I got to thinking about the off-road competitions coming up. Clyde, Jesse, Len, and Gary did the last two without me. We can't just… *not go*. Every December we come up with a new custom project so we can attract new business and these competitions are where we show them off. So attendance isn't optional.

I put Kali's Jeep back together with lots of cool custom options and then designed a lightweight off-road trailer to pull behind it. At first I was thinking this would be great for families. Little space to carry gear while on the trail. Gas cans, and water, and shit like that. Maybe a pop-up tent on the roof.

But most of the trailer was made out of aluminum and it was so light when I was done, I decided to turn it into a little camper instead. And then I thought… you know what? I bet people might like to eat a cupcake or two when they're out at these crawler competitions.

And oh, hey? Would this be the perfect way to advertise Kali and Alison's new baking business and give out samples on the trail?

So that's what I did. That's what I turned Kali and Kyle's Jeep into. A Custom Crawler Cupcake Creation.

The whole thing is teddy-bear blue. Which was not a real color before Clyde mixed up a special batch just for this occasion, but it is now.

It was a hit. Especially with Alison and Kali driving it around.

To say things only got better from there would be an understatement. Kali and Alison got their business off and running and Kali stayed in the city most days to bake. But she came to see me on the weekends. Or I went to see her.

But their six months is almost up at Alison's parents' house and I'm not gonna lie, I'm pretty excited about that.

So excited. Because Kali's parents gave her Kyle's house and helped her turn it into the perfect commercial baking kitchen. So she will be moving home and we won't be living in Kyle's house—or above the garage. Which means we're house-hunting now.

"What are you smiling about?" Kali asks.

"Just thinking about our future, that's all."

"Mmm-hmmm," she says. "Tell me again why we're at our parents' townhomes in the middle of the night?"

"You'll see," I say, leading her across the guest parking lot towards the woods.

"What?" She laughs. "What are you doing?"

"Just come with me. Kyle and I had a little chat about tonight."

"Did you now?"

I nod at her and smile.

After Kali told me that Kyle has secret messages for her I went looking for some on my app. It took me weeks to find them. Fucker. Wanted to make me work for this until the end, I guess.

But I did find them eventually. Just a few. Nothing like the cache he left for Kal. But the last one I found was an idea for a perfect date—should I ever get up the nerve to ask Kali out.

It makes me sad that he never got to see us together. I think he would've loved the idea. And while I don't need his date advice—at least not the way he intended it—I'm using it tonight for another reason.

"You're seriously taking me into the dark woods in the middle of the night in December?" Kali says.

"I really am," I say, giving her hand a squeeze.

"OK." She sighs. "This better be good."

I just smile. Pretty confident.

"OK," I say, once we enter the woods. "Don't let go of my hand. I wouldn't want you to trip over the tree roots."

"I can't believe I'm letting you do this."

"Just… come on," I say. "We're almost there."

"Where? There's nothing out here but—" She stops. Then gasps. "What did you do?"

"Come see," I say, tugging her by the hand in the direction of the light.

"Aiden Edwards!" Kali giggles. "You built me a fort!"

"Hell, I don't have skills like that anymore. I paid the local kids to help me."

We stop in front of the fort and admire it. It's more than a fort. It's practically a twig cabin. "Took us two weeks to weave the walls together. Then it rained, so the roof took longer. But that was a good thing because it reminded me that we needed a floor. They helped me lay down mats and build the fire pit. It even has a chimney."

"How in the world…"

"I told them they could play here after I was done with it. So they didn't mind. We never had a fort this nice when we were kids, that's for sure."

"No," she laughs. "We didn't. We had a few logs and used our imaginations for the rest."

"Yeah," I say. A little wistfully. Thinking back on the great childhood we shared in these woods. They were good enough though. All we needed back then. Just a spark to ignite our imaginations and carry us away to the land of kids.

But tonight is special. I have a question to ask her and I want everything to be perfect. The only way it could've been better is if I'd waited until summer.

But I couldn't wait that long. I need her to know that this thing between us is more than just a *thing*. It's forever.

"Come inside," I say, swiping away a curtain covering the front entrance.

"Oh, my God." Kali laughs, crawling through. Then she gasps and pauses. "What have you done?"

"Keep going," I say, getting on my knees behind her. We're all bundled up in coats and gloves. But inside there's no wind and there's a bed of straw on the ground. She scrambles inside and moves out of the way so I can follow her in.

"Let me light the fire," I say, crawling over to the fire pit and flicking my lighter to the kindling. "Then we can take our coats off and have a drink."

She glances around and spies the bottle of champagne chilling in a bucket of ice. She hands it to me and hugs her knees to her chest, smile so big I can see all her teeth. "You're incredible. And this is perfect."

"Almost perfect," I say, reaching for a wooden box where I have food waiting. "Can I make you a s'more?" I ask, unable to hide my laugh.

She laughs with me. "S'mores and champagne totally go together."

I pop the cork on the bottle, pour us each a drink in a plastic champagne glass, and hand her one. "To us," I say.

"To us." She sighs.

We sip, then kiss a little and eat s'mores. And it really does feel like we're kids again. Like life never happened. Like we're on summer break looking forward to fifth grade. Like we've got our whole lives ahead of us and Kyle is still here.

But he is here. Because this was his idea.

"Aiden," he said in that message. "Treat her like the pretty thing she was that day you met her. What would Kali, age eight, think was romantic? Then do that. Trust me, she'll love it."

"I have something to ask you," I say, once we're warm and settled. Our coats discarded in a pile in the corner.

Our shoes off and our bodies pressed up against each other.

Kali sucks in a deep breath and looks at me.

She knows. She has to know.

I take out the little velvet box and open it up so the firelight can dance its way across the diamond ring inside.

"Will you marry me, pretty thing?"

And then I get a kiss. And a "Yes," and more kisses.

I put the ring on her finger and we lie back. Relaxed and happy as we enjoy Kyle's perfect date.

Ready for what comes next.

I knew I would miss my brother on our wedding day. I knew it would be a hard milestone.

But I found a message from Kyle a few days ago. Hidden deep in the secret system called Dead Notes. Triggered by… I have no clue. Just… triggered by Kyle, I guess. Watching over me. Always ready to help me when I start to get sad again.

The baking business is going really well. Not only do Alison and I have quite a few regular online customers, but I bake bread and goodies for the restaurants and coffee shop in town.

Aiden and I moved in together several months ago. There was a townhouse for sale near our parents and it was just too perfect to pass up. I can't think of a better place to raise a family. Not that we're there yet, but who knows. After today I'll be Mrs. Kali Edwards.

But that can't happen until I get my dress on and walk down that aisle with my father.

Alison is here, bustling around like a manic bee as she bosses the women doing my makeup and hair.

"Don't mind her," I whisper to them. "This is her excited face."

I don't think they find Alison as endearing as I do, but hey. Can't please everyone. She is my people and we are good together.

"OK," Alison says, once I'm done with hair and makeup. "Dress time."

My mom is in here, and so is Aiden's mom. And the three of them help me with the dress. The tight, form-fitting bodice is woven with white pearls and the open back goes all the way down past my waist. Just thinking about Aiden placing his hand on the small of my back when we meet at the altar gives me chills.

But when the music finally starts and I take my father's arm to walk down the aisle, I'm not thinking about the dress.

My eyes are locked on Aiden and his best man.

Not Clyde, though Clyde is there.

But the empty space meant for Kyle.

It's really empty. We knew he'd want to be here so we made room for him.

And even though there was no wedding day message hidden in the Dead Notes, I don't need an app to let me know how Kyle feels about today.

When Aiden and I turn to face each other I lose track of everything but him. We say our vows and kiss, and when I turn to face our family and friends a buttercup falls out of my bridal bouquet.

I bend down to pick it up and show it to Aiden.

Because I didn't order any buttercups in my bouquet.

Aiden just plucks it from my fingers and tucks the tiny stem into my hair, then kisses me and whispers, "Thank you, Kyle," into my mouth.

And we take a little piece of our childhood and my brother into our new life.

The day my son is born I go looking for Kyle. I have left him hundreds of messages over the years since he passed and even though I ran out of his messages a while back I just know there's one more hidden in here somewhere. I press combinations of buttons inside the app trying to find it. Pound sign, O for operator, even 911.

But the one that finally unlocks that last final message from my best friend is… today's date.

I don't know what to make of that. I still don't believe in other realms, or ghosts, or anything like that. But I believe in us. I believe in Kali, Kyle, and me. And the bond we forged back when we were eight. I believe it's the kind of connection that lasts forever. That transcends life and death.

Maybe he just pushed a set of random numbers when he made the trigger for this message. Maybe he did some kind of weird calculation based on how long he figured it would take for Kali and I to realize we were in love, get married, and have a kid.

Or maybe… maybe he knew? Maybe he really did see something in the future and this is proof of the many unexplained coincidences that have happened since he died.

It's impossible to know for sure.

"You've reached Kyle," Kyle says. "OK, dude, this really is the last fucking message. You really need to let me go. But since you're here, poking around like a fiend who needs his fix, I'm gonna make good. One thing though—it's a choose-your-own-adventure kind of message. Ready? Press one if you married Kali and had a baby. Press two if you didn't. Go."

How did he do this? There's a little part of me that thinks someone else is doing it. Like… watching us or something and then adding messages as life goes on and milestones pass.

But it can't be anyone but him because it's *his* voice. It's really him.

I press one and wait.

"So," Kyle says, more subdued on this message than he's ever been in the past. "Married with a baby. Born today, I'm assuming. And let me guess. It's a boy and you named him Garfield."

I laugh, then whisper, "Dumbass," into the phone.

"All joking aside," Kyle says. "I just want you to know… I love you guys. And I know you're going to be happy. So tell little Garfield I said hello. And I hope he knows how lucky he is to have my two best friends as parents. I'll see ya all again one day. Not too soon, I hope. Love you, brother. Kyle."

The call ends. Like just cuts off, like this really is the last of the messages Kyle left for me. But then I have an idea. There's one more at least. The other option in my choose-my-own-adventure menu.

So I call back, repeat the process to gain access to the first message, and then, instead of pressing one, I press two.

Kyle comes on with a sigh. Then he laughs. "Fuck you, asshole," he says through that laugh. "Now you're just messing with me. Hang up the damn phone and go be with your wife and child."

And this time, when the call drops, I don't call back.

I just sigh as I gaze down at my son in my arms. Both Kali and the baby are sleeping and I don't want to wake them.

So I lean down and kiss my son on the forehead and say, "Welcome to your life, Kyle."

260

Welcome to the End of Book Shit where Julie gets to blab about anything she wants. If you're new to the EOBS (as we like to call it) then there's two things you need to know about it. One – it's never edited. I write these after the edits and proofs are finished. So you have to forget about all the fucks you give about typos when you read it. Second—I do have a tendency to ramble so sometimes they totally pertain to the book or the process and sometimes they don't. Also, I like to swear and generally just say anything I want. So if you're offended at the end, I don't apologize for that.

OK. So this book definitely didn't start out the way it ended. And I don't know why that surprises me anymore. After more than fifty books you'd think I'd get this by now. But every time I write the end I'm always surprised about how it turns out. I think this is why I have superfans who just read everything I write. I truly do go along for the ride with you guys.

OK, let me explain a few things about this book before I get to the all the really cool things that happened to this story while I was writing it, because things have changed for me as an author and I feel the need to clue you guys in.

Yesterday I wrote the EOBS for another book that will be releasing the last week in May. It's nothing like this book (but then again, it is. Kinda. Because I wrote it.)

But I say this for two reasons:

One – I wrote it under the pen name KC Cross. If you've been hanging out in my fan group or listening to the podcasts Johnathan McClain and I do (called Love Notes, BTW. You should really subscribe to it on iTunes) then you already know I've had this pen name in the works for several months.

Two – the reason I'm using a pen name is because this other book I just wrote that EOBS for is not Contemporary Romance, it's sexy Sci-Fi Romance.

Now you're probably wondering why I'm telling you this because a lot of you probably give no fucks at all about my new sexy sci-fi romance books. Here's why it's important:

First – you may have noticed this book is shorter than most of the other contemporary romances I've written. There's a good reason for that and I'll get to it in a minute. This book comes in right around 51,000 words. Even the shortest of my other books are at least 67,000 words. Most of them are over 80,000 words and almost all of my bestsellers are nearly 100,000 words.

I write fast. Very fast, actually. A leisurely writing schedule for me is about 2000-3000 words a day. So on that slow schedule I write a new book about once a month. 2000-3000 words a day is about three hours of work. It's quite a nice day. I get up early, knock out a chapter or two, then I spend the rest of the day doing other stuff not related to writing, but essential for the business of being an author.

I did this for about two years. Even last year when Johnathan and I were knocking out books almost every month this was my schedule. I'd write my chapter, send to Johnathan, and he'd do this thing and send the manuscript back in a day or two. In between our collaborative books I wrote five solo books too. But it was still a pretty kick-back schedule compared to the number of hours I spent writing from 2012 – 2016.

But I've kinda gotten a handle on this whole book-writing thing so in 2017 and 2018 I could write a book a lot faster than I could in the early days. I don't think I actually realized how good I'd gotten at pulling together a story and typing it up on my computer until this past January when I got an idea for a sexy sci-fi romance series.

If you know me as an author you know I only read science fiction books. The first series I ever wrote was new adult science fiction with a romantic subplot. But those books had a hard time finding an audience for a lot of reasons. Mostly because I had no idea what I was doing and they didn't fit neatly into a specific genre. They were fun, and cool, and well-written, but not a lot of people were looking for that kind of book.

So I switched it up and started reading and writing new adult romance. That's how I got my start. After that I spent a few years writing dark romantic thrillers and dark erotic psychological thrillers. And people loved the hell out of those. I love them too. I'm not gonna stop writing dark erotic thrillers, so if you're into them, don't worry. I have some cooking up in my brain this very moment.

But listen, I've written over fifty contemporary romance now and to be honest I need to write something else. So that's why I have the new KC Cross pen name and I'm writing sexy sci-fi romance. I'm not going to stop writing books like Pretty Thing or The Dirty Ones or 321 etc. I'm just going to do them a little different because even though I write fast, I can't write two 85,000 word books a month. I just can't. And I don't use ghostwriters. That is something I will NEVER do. I don't write books for the money. Believe it or not I have a lot of other talents that can pay my bills without the agony of pulling together a fictitious world filled with characters who feel real enough to keep readers coming back for more.

I'd been thinking about this pen name thing and going back to writing some sexy sci-fi romance for a few years and I even tried it out under the JA Huss name with the Anarchy Series. People loved it lot, just not *all* the people, you know? And that's not good for an author name because people stop trusting you to deliver the books they have come to expect.

Most of my fans pick up my books because they like the dark erotic thrillers I've been giving them for several years now. So I finished off the Anarchy series in late 2017 and went back to fulfilling expectations. And it was fine. It's fine. I'm super lucky because readers pick up my books every time without fail. I am the picture-perfect example of what a successful indie author looks like.

But… I'm starting to get bored, you guys. I'm not gonna lie. I need more than this if I'm going to continue being an author.

So in January 2019 I decided to make a change in order to feed my soul and keep my sanity. I decided that no matter what, I will make time to write sexy sci-fi (and some paranormal romance too) **in addition to** my contemporary romances. Because look, I love you guys. I want to keep giving you books. But something has to change and this is how I decided to do it.

In addition to my book writing career I now have a new career writing scripts with Johnathan McClain for TV. We just got offered a new deal with MGM to write a script for a TV show and that comes with lots of expectations, some of which I haven't yet fully internalized. Because if we sell this show after we write the pilot things will change for me in a big way.

So you see… my life is super full. And if I'm going to write books I need to write books that fulfill that elusive muse inside me that forced me to stop writing non-fiction in 2012 and start writing write fiction instead.

I do not want to stop writing contemporary romances. I feel connected to the stories I've told you over the years and I have a lot more inside my head that still need to be written. But I need to branch out and give this sexy sci-fi stuff a try.

So here's the main takeaway from this rambling EOBS—I have changed my writing schedule drastically in order to accommodate all the things I want to do. I am writing in two genres now and I will be putting out **one new book in both genres every month** for at least the next year. I write for 6-8 hours a day now, not because I have to, but because I *want* to.

But getting back to this book only being 51,000 words instead of 85,000 words – this is how I am able to make this change. I *can* write one 50K book and one 80K book a month. So if you're disappointed that this book is short, this is the reason why.

I'm not saying all my future contemporary romances will only be 50K. The story is the story and I will write it until it's complete. If that's 50K or 100K, doesn't matter. I'm not going to short you on the story to maintain some arbitrary word count limit. That's just not how I work.

But here's a good thing – all the shorter romances will also be cheaper. I have decided to put these shorter books on sale for $2.99 or LESS. So some of them will probably be 99c at times. AND they will be in Kindle Unlimited for the foreseeable future. That's good news for you and a decent trade off so we all get what we need out of this author/reader relationship.

So I hope you all understand why things have suddenly

changed in this book and what my commitment to you is going forward.

OK, now that that's out of the way I have some really cool things to tell you about this book, Pretty Thing. First of all, like I said, it didn't start the way it ended. I had originally planned to write a super sexy, super simple book with a "brother's best friend" trope. Which I did.

But then one day I was writing about Kyle's death and I remembered something from another book I wrote back in 2015 called Wasted Lust. If you've read the Rook & Ronin and Company series', then you know that Wasted Lust (also called Sasha's Book now) was the last book in those two merged series. Sasha was in the middle of a big crisis and called home to talk to her adopted mom, Ashleigh, for some advice. But her silly little brother, Five, picked up the phone instead.

Five is pretty famous in the JA Huss canon. He was born in the book Guns (Spencer's book) and makes appearances as a child in Wasted Lust and Happily Ever After. Then he shows up in The Misters and finally gets his own book at the end of that series called Five. He's also in the last book in that series, Mr. & Mrs.

But it's his part in Wasted Lust that's important here in Pretty Thing. The conversation with Sasha on the phone goes like this:

"Aston residence," Five says on the second ring.

"It's me, Five." I can almost feel him smile. "Is Mom there?"

"Sasha," he breathes in that all-knowing way, unnatural for a ten-year-old. "Did you know that we are leaving for New Zealand tomorrow?"

"What? Since when? I thought you were all going to look at colleges?"

"Since Ford—"

"You mean Dad." Ford hates it when Five calls him by his name.

"Whatever. He got a call to shoot a new pilot show."

"Oh, well, that's great, I guess."

"Great? Great? No, it's not great. Sparrow Flynn's birthday is tomorrow and Princess Shrike tells me they are having a party. I was not invited to this party, Sasha. And now my plans to crash it are ruined."

"Why the hell would you want to go to an eight-year-old girl's birthday party?"

"The Princess will be dressed up like a biker, Sasha. It's a biker theme and I have purchased her a leather jacket for the occasion. I wanted to be there to see the joy on her face when..."

I tune him out as I think about what the fuck is

going on at home. Princess Shrike's father—her real name is Rory, only Five calls her Princess—is world-famous custom bike builder Spencer Shrike. So this only makes sense in that context. And I don't even bother asking how he got his hands on a leather jacket fit for a nine-year-old. This is Five we're talking about. "I got nothing for that, Five. Can you get Mom?"

"How would you like to hear my proposal for my newest invention? I'm seeking early investors for my new technology app. I project that if a prototype can be developed in the next twelve months, we can go public in two years."

"Five," I say patiently. He's had a dozen of these ventures over the past few years. "You're ten years old. I'm not investing in your gaming apps."

"It's not a game this time, Sasha. It's an app that will change death as we know it."

"Morbid," I reply. "Get Mom."

"Morbidity has nothing to do with it. People will pay for years to have what I'm developing right now. A subscription that will last until infinity."

I don't really remember if I ever told you guys that the name of the app was Dead Notes, but it was. I've had that name in my head since I first penned that passage. In the Happily Ever After book Five is moving away to England to attend Oxford. This is a sad time for him and his Princess Rory because they are still kids and he was looking forward to going to high school with Rory and now he's off to college early because he can't hide his super genius smarts any longer to stay close to her.

And when he finally had to accept that he and Rory will be separated for years to come, he makes her an app called Love Notes. (Sound familiar? Lol Yes, that's also the name of the podcast Johnathan and I do about romance authors). And this app is a way to send love notes to each other while they are thousands of mile apart.

I put that Dead Notes thing in Wasted Lust for a reason. I knew that one day I'd write a story for it, I just didn't know when. And since I wrote that passage I have published more books than I can count, so I kinda forgot about it until I started writing about Kyle's death and the reading of the will.

That's when it hit me. Kyle bought the app some time in the past and these messages were all part of the legacy he left behind for his loved ones.

After that, this whole book changed in a new direction. This is what I love most about writing. Finding that one thing. That one special thing that changes your book form just another Brother's best friend trop-y romance into something completely different.

This is why I write books. For moment just like this. When my crazy mind puts two unrelated pieces of story together in a brand new way and what comes out is totally unexpected. This makes all the hard work and long hours' worth it.

I give no fucks how this book sells.

I give no fucks what the reviews say.

I love it. And Dead Notes is the reason why.

Ok, that's it for me. I hope you enjoyed reading Pretty Thing as much as I loved writing it. And I have two more books coming up real quick that follow this same pattern of "slightly taboo" topes. The next one is called Sweet Thing about a young girl and a much older man, and the third one is called Wild Thing about a spoiled princess who needs to be tamed by an alpha male.

It's not a series, *per se*, but they all revolve around something "slightly taboo".

AND—if you are into super sexy, super fun sci-fi romance please pick up my upcoming book, Booty Hunter, when it releases on May 27, 2019. If you fell in love with Rook & Ronin you WILL fall in love with this world and these characters too. Even if you're not into the sexy sci-fi stuff. I promise you. It's funny, and sad, and heartbreaking, and thrilling, and super, super erotic! My name will also be on the cover but the KC Cross name will be the "main author".

Until next time my special unicorn bitches—thank you for reading, thank you for reviewing, and I'll see you in the next book!

Julie

JA Huss

March 31, 2019

JA Huss never wanted to be a writer and she still dreams of that elusive career as an astronaut. She originally went to school to become an equine veterinarian but soon figured out they keep horrible hours and decided to go to grad school instead. That Ph.D. wasn't all it was cracked up to be (and she really sucked at the whole scientist thing), so she dropped out and got a M.S. in forensic toxicology just to get the whole thing over with as soon as possible.

After graduation she got a job with the state of Colorado as their one and only hog farm inspector and spent her days wandering the Eastern Plains shooting the shit with farmers.

After a few years of that, she got bored. And since she was a homeschool mom and actually does love science, she decided to write science textbooks and make online classes for other homeschool moms.

She wrote more than two hundred of those workbooks and was the number one publisher at the online homeschool store many times, but eventually she covered every science topic she could think of and ran out of shit to say.

So in 2012 she decided to write fiction instead. That year she released her first three books and started a career that would make her a New York Times bestseller and land her on the USA Today Bestseller's List twenty-one times in the next five years.

In May 2018 MGM Television bought the TV and film rights for five of her books in the Rook & Ronin and Company series' and in March 2019 they offered her and her writing partner, Johnathan McClain, a script deal to write a pilot for a TV show.

Her books have sold millions of copies all over the world, the audio version of her semi-autobiographical book, Eighteen, was nominated for a Voice Arts Award and an Audie Award in 2016 and 2017 respectively, her audiobook, Mr. Perfect, was nominated for a Voice Arts Award in 2017, and her audiobook, Taking Turns, was nominated for an Audie Award in 2018. In 2019 her book, Total Exposure, was nominated for a Romance Writers of America RITA Award.

Johnathan McClain is her first (and only) writing partner and even though they are worlds apart in just about every way imaginable, it works.

She lives on a ranch in Central Colorado with her family.